Wax Vainglorious: the Collected Works of li'l boy and Josephine's baby boy Volume 1; Envisioned by Vince Vanguard Vainglorious

by **Vince Rogers**

Vainglorious Press

A subsidiary of Vision Media Productions

1st Edition published by **Vainglorious Press**

ISBN: 978-0-615-25689-4
Copyright: © 2008 by **Vince Rogers**

United States of America

"The whole world is held together by the love and compassion of a very few people."

James Baldwin

Acknowledgements

Muses

In memory of my beloved Father, Mr. Charles "li'l Boy" Rogers, the best man I've ever known.

Mrs. Josephine Rogers-Lewis – My Beloved Mother

Mrs. Ruth P. Greene – My Beloved GrandMother

Dr. Brenda Joyce Greene – My Beloved Aunt

Ms. Terri L. Moreland-Bey – My Beloved Best Friend

Special thanks to: Valerie Rogers; Victor Rogers; Mrs. Gertrude Greene-Gordon; Ms. Effie Jane Rogers and Ms. Mary E. Parker for all of your inspiration

Motivators

In memory of Mr. Walter Gregory Butts, Our Beloved Family Griot.

Mr. Quinn Xavier Hood

Mr. Roland Lane Jr

Mr. Raymond V. Hayes Jr.

Ms. Vanessa Ayanna Moore

Mr. Edward "Buss" Johnson

Special thanks to: Jeff Diamond; Lejuano P. Varnell; Scott D. Lucier; Terrance Chatman and

my Yahoo! 360 "Friends" for all of your encouragement

Mentors

My Beloved "Professor-Confessor" Dr. Clifton E. Marsh; "A Man in Full"

Special thanks to Ms. Carol Stone-Taylor; Ms. Jacqueline Heard-Fields; Mrs. Verna P. Colson; Memphis Vaughan, Jr.; Rudolph Lewis; Andrew and Mark Anthony Rudder; Pamela Cole; Museum of the African Diaspora; Taj Mahal Review and Dr. Kathryn T. Gines for all of your support

Wax Vainglorious: the Collected Works of li'l boy and Josephine's baby boy **Volume 1;** Envisioned **by Vince Vanguard Vainglorious**

Table of Contents

This Girl I'm Fuckin'

Ain't got nobody to say *I love you* to right now

So this is dedicated to this girl I'm fuckin'

When she's gone, I kind of miss her

But mostly I miss her good dick suckin'

One day I'll settle down and change my marital status

Until then I'm satisfied with my li'l fuckin' apparatus

First met her one Friday night at this spot that cost a "dub"

No illusions about finding Miss Right off in this funky club

After my weak intro "Can you buy me a drink" was her opening line

Damn sure wasn't my rap, so I guess she thought I was fine

Don't get it twisted; I'm just a hard dick and some nuts to her too

She certainly ain't complainin', 'cus I eat that pussy like y'all other cats won't do

I like to suck on her clit and watch her jerk and try to pull away

I even love the taste and the smell of it; I could stay down there all day

Before I forget to mention it, this girl loves to give me long slow head

Sometimes she does this squirt thing, that scared me first time she fucked up my bed

I love it most when the coach sends number sixty nine in the game

The slob runnin' down my thighs and the taste of hot pussy shootin' flames

But nothing' beats straight up 1974 Boones Farm and Acapulco Gold style fuckin'

So to set the mood I burn some Black Love incense and put on "Keep on Truckin'"

I grab her by her firm thighs and pull her swiftly to the edge of the bed

As I stroke my hard dick against her pussy lips she throws back her head

Now her hot wet pussy is on fire and her nipples are hard as can be

After she can't take my pussy teasin' no more she moans "Ooooohhh - stick that dick in me"

I be strokin', I ain't jokin', tryin' to keep my balance from this good pussy and that weed I was smokin'

"I'm comin' I'm comin'!!!!" she screams and I can feel her walls throbbin' and that wet pussy soakin'

I lift her up on the bed with her ass shootin' up towards the moon

After I ride the pussy for a little longer we'll both be screamin' soon

"Oh Shit!!!!" we both cry out and fall limp and slump down to the mattress

I hold her close and stroke her locks and tresses - I don't love her, but I still like sweet caresses

I wish I had somebody to love, but so far in love I've had no luck in

So until that moment comes, I think I'll call this girl I'm fuckin

Vince Vanguard Vainglorious
Vainglorious Press 2005

Trio Dancers

Part I: Awakening

I tried going back to sleep, but once I'm up, I'm up. As I got halfway to the kitchen, I realized breakfast wouldn't magically be on the table this morning. That didn't seem to happen anymore, since Kedra moved out.

I looked in the fridge to see what was in there. There wasn't much, since I didn't have a chance to go to the grocery store this week. On top of everything else, I felt like I broke some kind of unspoken promise to Jesus by not to going to church today. I decided to split the difference and turn on the radio to the Gospel show on *WCLK*. *That'll work*. Reaching for the radio, the brightly flashing message light on the phone caught my eye. I scrolled through the Caller ID and saw that Kedra called seven times yesterday.

Kedra and I were together a little over three years. She had everything I should have wanted, but there was something missing. She came from a good family, she had a good job and she was fine as Hell. When I met her she was working at *Jomandi Productions* and I was designing their sets. We hit it off immediately and were living together before we knew it. We both know now that we moved too fast. I had decided it was time for me to stop looking for the "perfect" woman and I should see how far this relationship could go. As for her well – I'm irresistible.

I turned down my stereophonic church service after about an hour, so I could make my weekly call to my Mother in Baltimore. Hearing t*he Anointed Pace Sisters* in the background would at least keep her from asking me if I had gone to church. While I was talking to my mom, the phone beeped and I saw it was Kedra calling again.

"Is that your other line?" My Moms asked. I resisted telling her it was Kedra, because she wasn't her biggest fan. If she thought I was still talking to her after what she did, I would never hear the end of it. Of course my Mom didn't really need to know the details, before she began to make her feelings known about the situation.

"....Clif, baby, I know you think you loved that girl, but she just wasn't right for you....." Now when Mom gets going, about all you can add to the conversation is "Okay and Allright" I was still kind of tired and by now I was really hungry. I couldn't wait for my turn to talk again. "....Baby you're going to find somebody else, you're a good man and you deserve somebody good in your life."

Talking to my Mother always seemed to make me feel better, whether she was getting on my nerves or telling me things I needed to hear. On the other hand, if you didn't let her know you got her message she would go on forever. Finally my chance came as she took a breath to reload. "Okay Momma. I love you too. I'll talk to you soon."

I knew my Mother was right, but the way me and Kedra ended things really weighed on me. I told her we needed to spend some time apart. I felt it was the right thing to do, even though the relationship probably could have been fixed. The more we got into our careers, the less we seemed to talk about settling down or having a family anymore. I think we both still wanted that, but the more things we had to fill up the spaces in our lives, the less we seemed to need each other. Even though she had it all, I just never felt like she was "The One."

I decided I wasn't going to solve this great mystery of the universe sitting on the couch holding the phone. What I needed to do was get dressed and go get something to eat. Maybe if I would have gone to church this morning the answer would have come to me in a vision. As I was walking out the door, the phone rang again. This time I decided to answer.

"Clif, it's me…. How're you doing????... I saw your friend Keith at church….He said he talked to you a couple days ago…. I'm going out of town Monday, but I'll be back in time for your Homecoming concert….Can I see you before I leave????"

My instincts pulled at me to make an excuse not to see her, but I told her I was going to get something to eat and I could stop by on my way back. "That's fine" she said, "Can you pick me up some Jerk Chicken?" I guess that meant I was eating Jamaican too. Now it starts to come back to me why the fuck we broke up. The presumption of her request made me realize that I was probably making a mistake by going over there. Well I guess like the man sang on the radio this morning - *You got to go on and see what the ends gone be.*

Part II: My Old, New Room

Moving back to Atlanta has its pros and cons. On one hand, I'm close to my family. On the other hand, I'm close to my family. My Mother still treats me like a little girl. I'm ashamed to admit it, but I don't mind it that much these days. Besides, I'm living in her house for the moment so like she used to say *"As long as you live under my roof, you live by my rules."*

Usually when I wake up, she waits a few minutes before she comes out of her room and inevitably starts getting all in my business. Today is Sunday, so I assumed she would take the day off completely. Not a chance. Before I make it out of my bedroom door, damn if she didn't come out of the bathroom with her slip already on and rollers in her hair.

As she attempted to put on her other earring she exclaimed. "Cassandra do you know what time it is? Girl we gone be late!!!!" I had to collect myself before I spoke. "Late for what Mama????" I inquired. Now I had no plans today to be late, early or on time for anything. It's Sunday – for Christ's sake. All I wanted to do was sit on Mama's back porch with a glass of iced tea and try to figure out how the hell I ended up in her house again. Then I remembered.

I promised her I would go with her to church today. I remembered before she answered and said "What time does it start Mama?" I had to make a special effort not to attach the word Goddamn to my sentences today since it was Sunday. "Eleven o'clock. You remember don't you???? Has it been that long since you went to church????" She asked.

I took a shower in the other bathroom, and then went back to my old, new room to get dressed. As I sit on the side of the bed putting on my stockings, I try to remember if I really said I would go or if I just said I would let her know. Then I realized it didn't matter. She was almost dressed, it was already 10:17 in the morning and I'd never hear the end of it now if I told her I didn't want to go.

Now we both knew the real reason she wanted me to go to church. It was so she could see if there was any poor unsuspecting lame ass Junior Deacons she could try to palm me off on. Mama was "Old School". Since I was Thirty-Three and not married, she felt like I should wear a clearance sale sign around my neck at all times. Sometimes she made me feel that way too.

Mama never really forgave me for leaving Spelman after my sophomore year to move to Los Angeles. She was always the loudest one at every talent show I won. I can see her now hollering "That's my baby!!!!" at the top of her lungs, looking like that woman in the front row at the Apollo. She was there for me whenever I won a pageant and always made sure I got the best Easter speech at church. I thought she'd be happy for me when I announced I was leaving school to go to LA and follow my dreams, since she was always my biggest fan. I guess that shows how smart I really was.

She told me that yes I was good, but there would be lots of other people there who would be just as good. She said that a lot of people helped me get into Spelman, so I couldn't let her and them down. Although I understood where she was coming from, my heart was broken. All I could hear at the time was that she never really believed in my dreams at all.

Since Daddy died, Mama's social life revolves around weddings, funerals and her church. She goes to church mostly to find out about the next weddings and funerals. Her usual date for church is my Aunt Rena, but Rena said she had to take care of some "business" before church so she would be late. The church was full of people I vaguely remembered from childhood, but all of them seemed to remember me and spoke to me by name. I tried as best I could to remember all of the *Tom Thumb Weddings* and Christmas pageants they reminded me I was in. I was still as polite and poised with them as I learned to be all those years ago.

I figured some of these people were the people Mama said I let down, so it made me feel kind of obligated to tell them what they wanted to know. The ones who saw some of the commercial work or soap opera walk-ons I did in *Tinseltown* still seemed more impressed by my nine year old's rendition of *Going Up Yonder* at the Easter Pageant. Actually I remember that one too. It was the bomb. One woman did remember when I danced on stage with Tina Turner at the Oscars, but mostly everybody wanted to know if I was married, what was I doing now and if I planned to go back to school.

After Mama and I did all the catching up with these people that I could stand, I finally ushered her inside the church to find a seat. As we sat on the hard pews trying to look cute, Mama kept looking back and asking herself, but talking to me, "Now where is Rena????" Aunt Rena was my Mama's baby sister and her sidekick. They did everything together, which mostly consisted of shopping and watching TV while talking on the phone about shopping.

Sitting next to my Mama in church made me feel more like the little girl I used to be more than I care to admit. I had not been back to Ebenezer for quite some time. When I come here, I always feel like the Lord is going to tell my Mama about some of the things I wanted to stay buried back in Hollywood.

I often ask myself whether I would have gone farther if I had done some of the other things I refused to do. "Holly-Weird" turned out to be a lot tougher than I thought. I realize now that no matter whom I would have slept with or partied with, things probably would have turned out exactly the same. Damn, I guess mama was right all the time. So now I'm back here in Atlanta, listening to everybody tell me how good I was in *Purlie Victorious* twenty G-damn years ago, trying to figure out what I'm going to do next.

After church was over, we stood outside to speak to more people. We finally saw Auntie Rena. "Rena where you been girl???? I been looking all over for you." Mama asked. "Girl you know how that traffic is coming from my house." Rena said.

That dreaded Sunday morning traffic huh???? What's going on here???? Then I figured it out. Hiding in plain sight behind Aunt Rena was a tall, well educated looking, chocolate Brother who had *100 Black Men* wannabe written all over his face. Apparently scooping this fool up and bringing him to church with her was the "business" she was taking care of.

Without even speaking to me first, Rena announced his presence like we were at a debutante ball. "Cassandra this is Keith. Keith is from Bowie, Maryland. He goes to Flipper

Temple AME. He went to Hampton University. He's about your age. He told me he saw you on *Soul Train* one time and he wanted to meet you."

She made this morning announcement all in one breath. Apparently this clown with the cheesy ass grin works with Rena. I guess she showed him a picture of me or something. So the big plan for today was to bring him here with her to *"Club Jesus"* to hook up with me.

"Pleased to meet you" I said as polite as I could manage, fighting the urge to turn to Mama and Rena and cuss them out for this tired ass ambush. Keith and I chatted for a few minutes and tried to find some common connection between mutual friends who might have gone to Morehouse, Hampton, Howard or Spelman. He knew a whole lot of girls who went to Spelman. A whole lot. I knew mostly all of them hussies and tramps he mentioned, but I pretended not to. After a few minutes "Mr. Player, Player" gave me both his day job business card and his Noni Juice representative business card. Finally we exchanged "Goodbyes, Nice meeting yous and Hope I see you agains."

"I'll make sure she uses that card "My Mama whispered in Keith's ear as they hugged goodbye in Christian fellowship.

On the ride home Mama didn't say anything for a few minutes but smiled the slick smile of somebody who had unleashed a witty plot. They were serving dinner in Fellowship Hall after church and I was hungry since I didn't have a chance to eat breakfast. Of course Mama didn't want to go down there and eat anything. She has this thing about eating just anybody's food. Besides, she already did what she came to do.

Finally Mama started talking about the usual topics. The nice (in this case) sermon, how short Johnnie Mae's dress was and who's poor child was on crack now. Then as subtle as an elephant in the china department at *Macy's* "So what did you think about Keith????" She asked. "Not much" I said, hoping foolishly that the conversation would end there. How long had I known this woman????

Amazingly, her speech about my bad choices, getting my life together, finding a man, finishing school, making sacrifices for me and sometimes having to change your whole way around, was masterfully finished at the exact moment we pulled into the driveway. She also had some new scriptures she just heard to throw in for good measure. On the way home I learned that I was Thirty-Three years old, single, smart, pretty, had a lot of talent, living with my mother and needed to figure out what I wanted to do with the rest of my life. I love my Mama, she's a bloody genius.

I dropped her off at the house and told her I would be back shortly. Although I left because I didn't want to continue the conversation right now, I really did want to get something to eat. So I went to a Caribbean restaurant on Auburn Avenue that sold my favorite Brown Stew Shrimp.

I walked in and was pleased to see that it wasn't crowded. I could get my food, sit by myself and hopefully eat in peace while I tried to figure this shit out. There were only a couple of people sitting and waiting for their take-out, so I was able to walk right up and place my order. I walked away from the counter, found a seat and waited.

One of the men waiting for his order stood up, but instead of walking up to the counter, he walked toward my table. He looked vaguely familiar, but he seemed to have a touch of fear in his expression. He had a pretty stupid smile on his face too. *Oh Lord*, I thought to myself, *Who is this fool????*

"Cassandra - Cassandra Highsmith???? He said" As I glanced at him, a feeling of disconnected but pleasant familiarity came over me - or maybe I was just hungry. He was fine though. "Yes, do I know you?????" I responded with a slight bit of reproach, just in case he was some crazy psychic Brother who guessed my name or worse. "It's me Clifton - Clifton Broadnax" he said. That *Oh Lord* turned out to be more appropriate than I would have ever thought.

When I started attending Spelman, I met Clifton at a meeting for Freshmen who wanted to work on the Morehouse-Spelman coronation. Clifton was an Art major and an aspiring production designer. He was also a fine, dark, muscular Brother who was on the basketball team. We were both running around freshman year trying to make moves, do our thing and enjoy the little bit of freedom we had between curfews and studies. However, when we did spend time with each other or ran into each other, we would really, really talk.

We would talk for hours about any and everything. I had a boyfriend most of Freshman year, but he attended Tuskegee so I would never see him during the week. Clifton was a gentleman, a very serious student and an athlete, but more importantly he never had a shortage of girls around him. We did make a brief attempt at a relationship toward the middle of second semester Sophomore year, but he had to go home to Baltimore for the summer. By then I had already made the decision to move to LA. I didn't tell him or Mama about my decision, until I had already made plans to leave.

We both went up to the counter to get our orders, but I asked the cashier to change my order to go. We continued our conversation outside. At first it was awkward and nervous, but at the same time it was unexpectedly pleasant. I wasn't sure how Clifton felt about how we left things. I hadn't seen him since I left school. I sensed that I wanted to prolong the conversation much more than he did.

Although he seemed happy to see me, I got the feeling that if I would have stopped talking, he would have gotten in his car and driven away at any moment. I didn't want that to happen, but there was nothing I could do if he wanted to do the leaving this time. Then he said it. With a slight crack in his voice and a little moistness in his eyes he said "You know I really loved you girl. You broke my heart when you went away. Every time I saw you on TV, I would be so proud. I would always tell my girlfriend or whoever I was with, "*I went to school with that girl*" and I could tell they knew how I felt about you. I was so proud of you. So what brings a big Hollywood star like you to town???? Homecoming ain't until next week."

A million possible responses went through my head, but I simply responded "It was time for me to come home now." After we talked a while longer he gave me his business card and wrote his home number on the back. We gave each other a long hug and reluctantly managed to drive away. I wanted him to kiss me so bad I could taste it.

I walked through the front door of Mama's house with my container of Brown Stew Shrimp in one hand and my keys in the other. I placed my keys on the kitchen counter and the bag on top of the stove. Mama looked at me to see what type of mood I was in before she started back in on me. Much to her surprise I was smiling, so she smiled too. I would still hear it later, for going to get something to eat when I knew she was cooking dinner.

I placed my purse on the dining room table then pulled out the business card so Mama would see it. I gave her a long hug, and then I picked up the cordless phone off the charger and walked into my old, new room. "God is good" I could hear Mama say "God is Good."

Part III: Kedra's Journal

….I know it hurt Clif when he found out I had the abortion, but I honestly didn't think he would leave me. I wanted him, but I wasn't sure I should have the baby. I wasn't sure if we were going to stay together.

We were happy at first, for the most part. Although deep in my soul I always thought he was measuring me by some standard of a perfect woman that I could never live up to. It seemed like he was always searching for some ghost from the past. Then one night we were watching television and I saw the ghost with my own eyes.

He pointed out some girl on a rerun of *Living Single* who was playing Kyle's girlfriend. His eyes lit up like he was watching Venus Williams playing tennis topless against Serena in a thong. I asked him about her and he just said, *"I went to school with that girl."* I knew there was more to it, but I let it go.

When I met Clif, I knew he was the man for me and I wanted him. He was irresistible. I made sure I got him too. I saw him for the first time at the theatre. He looked so confident and in charge that I knew he was the kind of Brother I needed in my life. His business was getting more and more successful and running a struggling theatre company was demanding, so as time went on we saw each other less and less.

To be honest, I threw myself into work because as much as I loved that man, I wasn't sure if he loved me. Work was the only place where I was in control. Maybe the baby was exactly what we needed to keep us together. I'll never know now.

When he gets here I'm going to really let him know how I feel. I think I can accept it if he decides not to be with me, but I'm going to give it everything I've got. I even went to church today and prayed about it. I just got off the phone with him and he's supposed to be bringing me something to eat. Maybe I should have cooked. They say that's the way to a man's heart.

I'm going to let this man know exactly how I feel about him. I'm not going to play any more games. If he can't accept me for who I am then I guess it's not meant to be. It's time for him to stop chasing that ghost. Maybe I should call my Mom before he gets here. *Oh Lord, I hope you heard my prayers.*

Kedra

Vince Vanguard Vainglorious

Vainglorious Press 2006

NationTime!!!!

....Hmmm, I wonder what they'll be begging us for this time. They've lost most of their power, but they haven't lost any of the arrogance....

"Sir the President of the Americas is here to see you." The receptionist announced.

"This time does he have the Cuban cigars I asked him to bring????"

"No I don't think so. I guess he forgot them again" She replied with a wry giggle.

"OK, let his ass wait a while then."

Memoirs: September 14, 2035

One day when I was in primary school reciting the Pledge of Allegiance; I wasn't so much stuck on the words that make up the pledge as I was the word allegiance itself. *Allegiance ~ Loyalty or the obligation of loyalty, as to a nation.* It was obvious to me at a very early age that it didn't include "…liberty and justice for all." That was well - elementary. With all the flag represented, the question for me was did I ally myself with what that flag stood for???? The answer at the time was obvious to me - No.

So then the question became, "Well what do I stand for. What do I believe in" For all of my life the only option ever presented to me was the Great American Dream a la Martin the King, but for some reason I only dreamed of having my own thing. Would my forefathers who suffered the whips sting, want me to believe in any other thing. Damn, I'm a poet and I didn't even know it.

Mental Note: My School Days – circa late Post Jim Crow Era, P.O. (Pre-Obama)

"…We refer to this sound as a Tarzan yell. This class concludes our discussion of African history…." The schoolmarm pronounced definitively.

Memoir: September 14, 2035 (continued)

I once saw a picture in a Life Magazine of little African kids going to school. They had on navy blue short pants, crisp white shirts and blue and orange rep ties. They looked so European that I could imagine their British accents jumping off of the page. I was looking rather Euro-American myself in my Izod shirt and some Calvin Klein jeans. Yet I always remembered how I was affected by the man wearing the blue Dashiki who brought the big drums to class for show and tell. I was so excited by the soul stirring sounds they made, that the teacher had to tell me to stop acting a like a fool and quit dancing. I felt something that at the time, I didn't really understand. Something shall we say - Behind the Music.

As much as everybody tried to literally and figuratively beat the Black out of me, I always felt the call of that drum, even though there was no place for it in my world of advanced placement classes, debutante balls and Baptist church junior usher boards. So I made good grades, did what I was told, stayed in school and didn't act a fool. I finally marched down the graduation aisle and that Summer I partied a while. Then I went to "the House".

Here I would try to make my mark amongst the most progressive young minds our race had to offer to the world. "....Dear old Morehouse...Dear old Morehouse..."

"....Can you tell me how to get to the Liberation meeting my Brother?"... "Naw man, but I can show you how to get to the career placement office."... "I am sad to announce that Jesse Jackson will not be speaking tonight because we could not pay his fee....On a brighter note there will be a CIA job fair after chapel services have ended, so please tuck in your Africa medallions... and don't forget the Greeks are stepping tonight."

The Greeks are coming!!!! The Greeks are coming!!!! Maybe I read the wrong brochure.

I put away my memoirs so I could get back to work. "Allright Boomqueshia, send that fool in. "I pronounce into the royal intercom.

"President Blush, the Emperor will see you now." She informed him.

When he walked into my office I couldn't help but notice how much he looked like his dumb ass Grandfather, except he didn't look quite as bright.

"Thanks for meeting with me your Majesty; I see you Niggers are still doing OK for yourselves"

"No shit, leaving you Crackers was the best move we ever made"

"So I guess y'all wouldn't consider coming back, huh???"

"Not even if you paid us this time. "I say with pride.

"Well you know there'll always be some low paying jobs and second class citizenship waiting for you whenever you change your mind." He said with a big smile.

"God Bless the Americas." I replied in all sincerity.

We both let out a hearty laugh over that one. After we finished the large bucket of our favorite extra spicy, extra greasy, dark meat *Church's Chicken* that I had shipped over for him, he wiped his thin lips and asked.

"Be honest boy, did you ever really dream you Niggers could set up your own governments that address your own unique concerns, develop your own thriving economies, break away from the illusions of Christianity and create your own nations where Black people could unashamedly embrace your own cultures????"

"Always" I said with pride. "Always"

I could tell that wasn't the answer he was hoping for. I could tell he really didn't believe me. Yet, it was the only answer I could honestly give him. As I thought about all of the marvelous things we as a people had accomplished in such a short time, I couldn't wait to tell him about this year's record watermelon crop.

"Okay let's get down to business, you ole Peckerwood. What can we do for you????" I ask.

"Well "My Nigga", I'll get right to the point. What we need from you right now is...."

Vince Vanguard Vainglorious
Vainglorious Press 2007

Mojito Sunset

I am awakened by a gentle stroke across my forearm. As the last fragment of a dream set in America escapes through my eyes, I look to my left and see the face of the weathered but graceful old Cuban woman sitting next to me. She begins to come into focus as she leans across me slightly to get a better view through the small window.

She has the look of someone falling in love all over again with someone she has not seen in quite some time. She looks at me softly and points her finger towards the vista. She only utters one word - "Havana." As I look at her and smile quaintly, I have the strange feeling that I will soon love this yet undefined vision as much as she does.

The cab driver dropped me off at the Hotel Lincoln in less time than I thought it would take to get there. I would find out later that I paid him way too much for the privilege. I didn't mind. I was just happy to get to the hotel without any trouble. I was eager to start my adventure. Besides, I figured out early on in my journey that cab drivers in Havana were very good people to know.

"Adios, Amigo!!!!" He shouted as he sped away down the decaying narrow boulevard to rejoin the day's festivities.

After I settled into my room, I decided to take a walk around the city. Since I don't speak much Spanish, I figured it was a good idea not to stray too far from the hotel.

Besides, I had no idea where I was headed. No sooner than I stepped through the threshold onto the sidewalk, did a copper complexioned beauty in an old, yellow, gingham dress, walk up to me. She appeared seemingly from out of nowhere, as if she sensed I needed a guide.

"You like chica????" She inquired in Spanglish.

I was intoxicated by my new surroundings and she was quite lovely, but I managed to sober up long enough to reluctantly reply "No gracias." I do like chicas. I like chicas very much, but I was taken aback by her abruptness and couldn't think of a more appropriate response at the time. She just smiled at me as if she knew she'd see me again.

As she turned and walked down the avenue, I couldn't help but notice her magnificent figure. She walked with a gait that was somehow dainty, yet athletic. Still it also had both military-like precision and feminine power. Her legs were not long, but they were muscular and strong. Yet they also looked voluptuous and soft. She filled her dress almost to overflowing – front and rear, but there wasn't an ounce of fat on her. Her breasts were round and delicate. Yet as she walked her chest bounced and heaved with confidence and pride.

She stopped a short distance down the boulevard to talk to a few ladies gathered under a lamppost across the street. Looking at her heavenly form and bronze skin glowing under the light of the half lit street lamp and the purplish red hue of the sunset, it gave me pause as to whether I should have accepted her advances. Alas it was too late; we had gone our separate ways.

I walked in the other direction making my way along the Malecon. From what I read about it in the Michelin guide, I figured I could use it as a landmark to find my way back to the hotel if I got lost. As I walked along the seawall, I was captivated by the sun glistening on the water as it took its nightly fall from the sky. It was a magical sight.

Yet if you looked beneath the surface of the water, it didn't look fit to drink let alone to swim in. Nevertheless, a boisterous group of energetic teenagers jumped into the murky green agua seemingly without the slightest fear of the mortal consequences. They were bold and strong like their ancestors, possessing no fear of foreign bacteria or parasites.

Couples young and old strolled along the sidewalks or sat on benches immersed in lively conversation. I stood in awe of the breathtaking beauty of my new environs. The romantic sun, the tropical scenery, the Caribbean breezes, it was so beautiful it almost seemed evanescent. By the way, did I mention the beautiful women I saw????

The women, coming from town or market or work, walk miles on cobblestone streets in high heeled shoes with their backs straight as boards, gliding on legs that glow like bronze pillars. Yet they never falter or fail. Cuban women are hot and cool at the same time. They ooze sexuality, while simultaneously they command respect. They have a certain poise that makes them all the more beautiful. I was as captivated by their full switching hips and long batting eyelashes as much I was touched by how they bore their endless struggles and countless burdens with dignity.

The old women are just as beautiful. Yet they are possessed of a certain melancholy that is not found in the young. They teeter through the streets carrying heavy bags in their hands and the weight of yesteryears sacrifices on their backs. I watch an old lady stoop slowly to play with a baby in her path. The innocent child caresses her wrinkled skin as if tracing the history of their country in the lines of her face.

I become so swept up in my new surroundings that I didn't notice that the chica from the hotel has been following me. "You no like chica????" she asks with an impish smile as she sidled up next to me. I maintained the same puzzled look, as her questions continued. She asked simple questions and the English I could understand, but I couldn't manage to answer any of her inquiries. Where was this leading????

Against my better judgment, I didn't rebuke her or try to get away. In the back of my mind, I was anticipating some picaresque accomplice to appear out of nowhere with a shiny stiletto and demand my meager purse. I took a quick look around and realized there was no lurking lothario about. Since my senses supported that I wasn't trapped in a bad Hemingway novel, I decided to play along.

"You like mojito????" She inquired as she made the universal hand gesture for knocking back a few stiff ones. "We go drink the mojito, Okay????" She announced while grabbing my hand without pause for refusal.

We proceeded towards the city, heading away from my desired path. I had no idea where we were going, but strangely enough, I wasn't worried. Apparently I am on a date now with a mysterious bronze beauty whose name I don't know, I have no idea where I am or how to get back to my hotel. I have no idea whether this story is going to wind up in my journal or if I'm going to wind up giving a statement to La Policia. Or even worse - who would claim by body here in Cuba???? I was relieved that we didn't wander off very far before we reached our destination.

Approaching the interior of the city, I am fully aware now that I am most certainly in Havana, Cuba. I am in the home of Che, Fidel, Matos, Cienfeugos….La Revolucion!!!! The posters, signs and billboards are constant reminders of the victories of the people. Why didn't anyone tell me there would be a Chinatown?!?!?!?!

Amidst the worn pastel Spanish facades and the ever present specter of revolution ….there is a Chinatown. I have found the one thing that every nation has in common. Chinatown, where fifty year old fat European men share ice cream sundaes with fifteen year old veteran working girls. Chinatown, where authentic Cuban food is sold by Spanish speaking women in authentic Chinese gowns. Chinatown where I walk insouciantly with my new companion under the glow of paper lanterns that are decorated in festive indifference to their Communist origins, yet made in Taiwan. Even the Siamese cat lying in the windowsill looks amused.

We take a seat inside the first bar we come to in ole Cuban Chinatown. My companion starts to shimmy in her seat and sings "Mojito, Mojito." like a little American girl anticipating the arrival of birthday cake or a new doll. *What the hell is this mojito????* I ask myself. Obviously I can't answer the question myself, so I ask the waiter. He speaks little English, but immediately he fills up with delight when he hears the magic word.

"Ah, the Mojito. The Mojito is the sun, Amigo. The Mojito is the water of life, the fruit from the trees. The Mojito is strong like a man and sweet like a woman. The mojito is Cuba my friend."

Finally, the waiter brings the drinks and seems as happy to serve them as my companion is to finally imbibe the much anticipated elixir. She takes a long sumptuous swallow as I take my first cautious curious sip. After only a few minutes or so, "Two more mojitos!!!!" I yell to the waiter. I would continue to sing this chorus in between our care free talking and singing and laughing and dancing, into the night.

After much resistance to my insistence, I finally convince my date that we should leave while I am still able to walk back to the hotel. As the cacophony of lively sounds continues to filter in from the avenue outside, I manage to fumble to pay the bill. I think the waiter is happy with his tip, but I am too intoxicated to tell.

We stagger into the streets and dance our way towards the Malecon. Wobbling and teetering along we make a spectacle of ourselves as we navigate our way down the avenue along the seawall. For a little while the ever present reality of civilian spies in the crowds, government soldiers on every corner and paid informants lurking in the bars is lost on us. To my surprise, in the distance I see my old friend the cabdriver Jose approaching. He is a sight for sore eyes, throbbing feet and spinning heads.

"Amigo, I see you find chica" He said.

"No Jose, I think chica find me" I tell him.

"I see you find Mojito too" He detected from my wobbly legs and the bittersweet smell of my breath.

"I definitely found the Mojito" I say clutching onto my date for the evening for support as we spill into the cab.

Yes I had found mojito after mojito after mojito and now my huevos were scrambled. I couldn't wait to get back to my room. I was jolted awake by Jose, as the cab came to a screeching stop. We had finally reached the hotel after what seemed like days.

Apparently my date had already exited the taxi somewhere along the way. Somehow she also managed to find my wallet without waking me. She paid the cabdriver and kept a little for herself. It was less than I would have paid a guide, but certainly more than I am used to paying a drinking buddy. I didn't mind.

"Adios Amigo!!!!" Jose yelled as he sped off into the night in search of his next wayward voyageur.

A few days later I made my way back to the Malecon to sit on the seawall and gaze at the dusky purple sunset. I must admit that I was hoping to run into the beautiful bronze chica again. If only to assure myself that the other night wasn't just a wonderful dream. If I was to see her again it would not be today.

I sat and watched a long legged, young, onyx complexioned woman stand and stretch her flawless arms toward the sky, following an evening of sunbathing on the jagged rocks. She peeked at me out of the corner of her eye and shrugged off my glances at her bikini clad perfection without a care. I couldn't help but wonder if she liked mojitos???? As she gathered up her belongings in her towel, I suddenly became fixated on the moon in apogee as it approached its position over the old Spanish fort in the distance that once protected Old Havana.

Vince Vanguard Vainglorious
Vainglorious Press 2006

Facts of Life: A Family Vignette

As he looked with admiration upon his maturing 13 year old son's wiry muscular frame and his lovely 15 year old daughter's budding bosom and widening hips, he realized that he would finally have to have "The Talk" with them soon. Although he wasn't sure how to approach it.

He had no previous experience with such things and did not remember having such a talk with his parents at all. He decided that the best way for him to approach this delicate and potentially life altering conversation was to sit down and reflect on his own sexual experiences over the years and focus on what he had learned from them.

During these hours of reflection, he realized that sex meant something different for boys and girls altogether. The consequences that resulted from being sexually active affected them differently also. He was very serious about providing his two burgeoning young adult children with the most meaningful and relevant information that he could make available to them. This required careful considerate thought and he was determined that he would not broach the subject with them until he knew exactly what to say.

One evening while he was sitting and pondering the issues of sex and the mysteries of sexuality, his son and daughter appeared before him unexpectedly. They both had the same aporetic look on their faces. He could tell that they had something important to ask him. Possibly it was even worse. Did they have something serious to tell him????

His daughter was a lovely wisp of a thing and a bit shy. Just as he expected, she would not be the first one to divulge what was on their minds. However his son was a brash bold strapping young lad. He was not one who was given to holding his tongue and always spoke his mind.

"Dad, we've got some questions to ask you because we've been hearing a lot of different things from our friends about sex." He said to his father in his most maturely serious and deep manly voice. "We think it's time for you to tell us straight up about the "Birds and the Bees." Okay?!?!?!?!"

The father, who was sitting in his favorite chair, tilted his head up slowly from his Essence Magazine. He looked over the top of his reading glasses at them quizzically, yet he was also somewhat relieved. He was so proud that his bright young creations had come to him for answers.

Yet at the same time he was very concerned about sharing this new and powerful knowledge about sex with them and the affect it could have on their lives. He pressed his finger against his temple and rested his firm jaw upon his hand for a moment. He began to think some more about what he would say to them. After a few more moments of reflection, he decided it was now finally time to dispense his well considered and sage advice. "Son, pull down your pants and show your sister your thing" He said.

"Daddy!!!!" His delicate young flower of a daughter exclaimed "I've seen his little thing before. We used to take baths together when we were little. Remember???? My

God!!!! I don't want to see that little thing."

Her father slowly rose from his chair. He looked his baby girl straight in the eyes. He gave her a look that only a Daddy could give. She knew he meant business.

"That is the only one of those things you've ever seen, Right????" He asked with a gentle sternness. "Oh my God Daddy!!!! Yes, that's the only one I've ever seen. What's wrong with you today????" She shrieked.

"Well good then." He said. "Because let me tell you right now, them things don't do nothing but make you fat. They're a big pain in the ass. They try to make a sucker out of you every time. Every time you see one coming, you're going to have to clean up after it. You hear me girl?!?!?!?!"

The young lady was now so perplexed and bewildered by what she just heard that she couldn't speak a word. When her dear father asked her to raise her skirt and show her brother her's she barely heard him, but she did as he asked without question like any good daughter would.

"Now boy" he admonished his son "You see that thing there???? That thing right there'll take all your money. I mean every goddamned penny of it. It won't leave you any time to play with your friends or play by yourself. Every time you think you've got it licked, it'll just leave a bad taste in your mouth. It'll always have you going to the doctor. It'll even have the government taking money out of your paycheck. Do you hear me boy????"

His two lovely children affirmed that they indeed had both heard him loud and clear and would heed his every word. As soon as he finished, they quickly asked if they could go to their rooms now. As they ascended the staircase to their rooms, they kept their eyes fixed on their father the entire time.

Their father was so very touched by his children's reverence and admiration. His fears eased, he resumed reading his article about "25 Ways for Professional Urban Women to Prevent Yeast Infections from Milan to Milwaukee." Soon he would retire to his chambers for a good night's sleep. He was sorry his wife missed this most important moment, but her job as a V.P. at the bank required that she sometimes work late at night with her boss.

Dear old Dad was relieved that they finally had "The Talk." Now his kids wouldn't have to pick up a bunch of bad information out in the streets. In the years to come he would often take pride in the fact that his kids never had any other questions for him about sex. In fact, they were such good kids that he couldn't remember them needing to ask him for his advice about anything ever again. *"Those two are gonna be just fine,"* he often said to himself. *"Just fine indeed."*

Vince Vanguard Vainglorious

Vainglorious Press 2007

What's In the Blood....

....Cicero Avenue is on fire tonight. There's a lot of money to be made out here. The "Po-Pos" are rolling heavy too. A lot of tricks are still out here creepin'....

....The cops know me. They might fuck with me just for standing outside this car. I have to decide right away to either get in or walk away. I might as well get in....

I recognized his face as soon as I stuck my head inside the window. I didn't have time to be shocked though....but I was. He didn't seem to recognize me at all, so I decided I might as well get in the car. Money is money and a dick is dick I always say.

I didn't expect to smell that sharp stench though. There was an open pint of *Glenmore* gin stuck between his legs. He seemed a little nervous or something, but not the kind of nervousness that a first time trick has.

I didn't want to be the first person to say anything. I thought he might recognize my voice. On the other hand, I don't know why I thought I was important enough for him to remember me.

We rode around for about a minute before anybody said a word. It was just a minute, but it seemed a lot longer sitting in the silence. The kind of guy that didn't say anything usually scared me. Sometimes, I might even ask him to let me out of the car.

He took a couple of big swallows from the gin bottle while he drove, which was usually a really bad sign. Dudes like that are usually fucked up in the head, too rough with you or they want to come all in your face and shit like that. I knew him though, or at least I remembered who he used to be.

His *Infiniti* looked clean, but I could tell it was kind of old. It smelled like he had already been fuckin' in it before he picked me up. It smelled more like ass than pussy too. That's cool with me if that's what he's into. It's just gonna cost him more money.

The music was turned down really low. It seemed like he wanted you to hear it, but he really couldn't stand listening too it himself. He was listening to *WGCI* but you could tell it wasn't really his flavor.

The creepy silence and the muffled bass were starting to put my nerves on edge. I really needed a cigarette. It didn't look like he let people smoke in his car, so I decided not to ask him. Somebody had to say something soon though.

I decided I would at least ask him to roll down the window. A nice summer lake breeze would feel good right about now. At the very least it might blow the smell of funky ass and cheap liquor out of the car. I cleared my throat so I wouldn't sound nervous or scared before I asked him.

"So what's your name????" He asked before I had a chance to say anything.

Apparently he didn't recognize me, which made me feel a lot better. I think he was trying to make his voice sound "Ghetto". I guess he wanted me to think he was from the streets or something. Even if he wasn't using the fake voice, he still didn't sound like the man I remembered. He sounded like he was lost, but not the kind of lost where you just need to ask a stranger for directions.

It had been some years since I'd seen him so maybe it wasn't even him. When I looked over towards him there was no mistaking his face. I also glimpsed the Chicago Public Schools parking decal on his windshield. There was no mistake about it. Principal Hampton. *Damn.*

Money is money and dick is dick, I had to remind myself. I learned a long time ago that there ain't any real heroes in the world. I know people are just people, but Damn - Principal Hampton????

Back when I was at *Clemente* he was my Homeroom Teacher in 9th and 10th grade. They made him Assistant Principal the next year. That was the year I had Lakeisha and dropped out of school. He really made homeroom fun. It only lasted thirty minutes every day, but Mr. Hampton was a really cool teacher. He was especially cool with the girls. He never called roll, he let us eat in class and do our nails. If you got in trouble, rarely would he call your Mama. He would always tell us that we were little Kings and Queens. He would tell us that we could do anything if we put our minds to it and stayed true to our selves. He even called me smart and told me I was pretty.

He said I should go out for Majorettes one day. He told me I should do something in fashion because of how sharp I dressed. He even said I should think about going to college.

Mr. Hampton had this little thing he always used to say. He would say that *"What's in the blood has got to come out."* I never really understood what it meant though. I think it meant that since we came from Kings and Queens we should treat each other like Kings and Queens or something like that.

"My name is *Diamond.* What's yours????"

"*Roberto.* You can call me *Rob* though."

Damn. I knew he wasn't going to use his real name, but damn….Roberto. *Roberto Clemente High School*, now those were the days. That's what people usually say about high school, because of the pep rallies, proms, football games and boyfriends and shit. For me - back then I was mostly doing just about what I'm doing now.

Before I had my baby, I always had everything I ever needed. Boys usually gave me everything I wanted. I wasn't abused by my Daddy or molested by my Uncles and I wasn't put out on the street by my Mama either. I just like fuckin'. I like money. I like fuckin' and money.

I started having sex when I was about twelve. It's just something that happens when you're always over at somebody else's house and your Mama ain't never at home. The first time was just some older boy that I don't really even remember now. By the time I was about thirteen, I looked about eighteen, so the li'l *"Corner Boys"* were always trying to get with me. At first, I would let almost any one of the cute ones just have some pussy. Sometimes they would buy me something to eat without me even asking or pick me up from school so I wouldn't have to ride the bus home.

I noticed that if I said "No" to the little ugly ones though, they would start trying to give me stuff. They said they would buy me a gold bangle or some earrings or just give me some money if I gave them some. Most of the time, the ugly ones could fuck way better than them *"Pretty Boys."* After I realized that, I started getting money from the cute ones too. Once I got older I realized that it didn't matter what they looked like. If it didn't make dollars it didn't make sense. All that other shit they gave me either got broke, my Mama took it, or I just lost it anyway.

"Can I smoke in your car????"

"Yeah, just roll down the window."

Li'l fast tail Tamika Scott. I guess it's like my Mama always said *"What's in the blood has got to come out."* I remember when she was in school. Her skirt was always just a little bit higher and her tops were always just a little lower than the other girls. She was hardly a dumb girl, but I never heard her talk about anything but boys. I used to hear them talk about her too. Mostly, I would hear the other girls talking about how she liked to suck dick and who they would see picking her up from school. They used to call her Mama a "Hood Hooker" whatever that means. She was in my class up until I got the promotion, then I never saw her much after that.

"So what's up with you tonight???? Wit' yo' handsome self. A man like you must really be horny to be riding around over here in this nice car????"

"I'm just out trying to have some fun."

Flattery will get you nowhere. The truth is this wasn't any fun for me at all. I didn't even want any pussy and I wasn't horny anymore. I had already fucked a little *"Hot Boy"* I met a while back at this club down on *South Halsted*. For me, he was everything that *"Miss Thang"* thought she was. Black "Roughneck" slim tall young Nigga, with a tight little ass.

I know it might sound crazy, but I felt like I couldn't just go straight home after that. Every time I fucked around on Melissa, I felt like if she finally caught me she could at least understand it if I told her it was a woman. So after I "got my freak on" I usually picked up a little "trick" on the way home just to put things back in order.

I like women. I like men. People think it's all about sex. All about booty. All about pussy. I like pussy. I like a man to hold me too. Women think it's all about the size of your dick. I'm packing ten inches, so a small dick ain't my problem either. I'm all man. I have the knee operation from my football days to prove it. If that really means anything. I've got the rug burns on my knees to prove it too. If that really means anything. I'm not a bottom or a top. I'm not on the "Down Low" either. I'm just who I am.

"So are you married?????"

"No."

I am a liar though. I met my wife Tracy at the *"Greek Picnic"* in Philly back when we were still in college. I was just hanging out with a bunch of my frat brothers. We ran into some AKAs that one of the brothers knew from *Lincoln University*. I started talking to Tracy just to look like I was down with the program. After that, when we would road trip up to Lincoln to see the "Bros", she would always make sure I had a place to crash.

We became good friends, but we lost touch for a while after we graduated. When she moved to Chicago to work for Chapman and Cutler, she got in touch with me through one of her Sorors. She was so into her career that she was hardly ever around. She was the perfect girlfriend for me. So we started dating and the rest as they say is history. Well it's not quite history yet.

"Turn right down this next street. I know a good spot."

"You live over here????"

"I stay all the way over on 103rd. You don't wanna go all the way over there do you????"

"I do if you've got your own place"

I don't usually take "tricks" to my house. I don't like everybody in my neighborhood knowing all of my business. Ain't no shame in my game. I just usually go somewhere else to do what I do. It was getting late though so at least I wouldn't have to find a way home. I guess I can trust him. If he did anything crazy, I'd just tell him I knew who he was. I hope he knows that if we go to my house it's gonna cost him extra though.

"Yeah I guess that's cool. It's just me and my little girl, but she's staying over at my Cousin's house tonight."

"That's cool then. You gotta show me how to get there."

I already knew exactly how to get there. I know plenty of "Banjee Boy" faggot "Gayngstas" who stay on that side of town. As I made my way towards her house, I tried to imagine what her place was gonna look like. Typical "ghetto fabulous" I suspected.

The stained light blue shag carpet. The cheap woodgrain entertainment center with the big screen TV. The different Daddy lookin' baby pictures all over the place. The beige walls covered with yellow weed smoke stains and faded roach spray spots. The smell of old collard greens and pissy sheets hanging in the air. Trust me - I'd been there before. It was pretty obvious by how she'd taken to her chosen profession that she'd probably be there forever.

"It's right around the corner. Don't park right in front of my house though."

"Okay, just show me where."

I always thought he was a "sissy" to tell you the truth. Back in school he would get along really good with the girls, but he was kind of hard on the boys. He would encourage the girls to run for the SGA or class Queens or go out for cheerleading, but he never said much to the boys except to study and try to make something out of themselves. Maybe his Mama and Daddy were real hard on him or something.

Don't get me wrong he was cool with everybody, but he just seemed to be more interested in what the girls were doing. Even though we were too young, you'd still catch the other male teachers taking a peak at our booties. Whether they were trying to fuck the little girls or not, they still looked. We just figured that's the way they are I guess. Expect for Mr. Hampton.

"Park right over there, up under the streetlight. That'll keep anybody from messing with your car."

"You sure there ain't anybody else at your house. I see a light on????"

"Honey please, ain't nobody gonna mess with you or your car. I stay by myself. Please believe. This neighborhood ain't that bad. As long as you don't mess with nobody, ain't nobody gonna mess with you. Don't be scurred" She said jokingly.

Shit, I can't tell. It's was late, but some people were still sitting out, even more were standing out and a couple of people were on the ground layed out. If anybody tells you that capitalism has abandoned the ghetto, just drive through the right neighborhood at the right time of the day. Everybody from the old lady sitting on her front porch to the teenagers standing in front of the convenience store stay tuned in to see if there might be any economic opportunities.

In the old days, vendors would walk through this neighborhood pushing their merchandise around on carts. They would shout out what was for sale at the top of their lungs. ....*Watermelon Man!!!!.... Rag Man!!!! ....Ice Cream Man!!!!.... Coal Man!!!!....*

Tonight the "DopeBoys" keep their merchandise hidden in the cracks of cinder block walls and under their Mama's front porch. They whisper out their inventory stealthily to see if anyone within earshot may have need. *"....I got that hard....I got that powder....I got that kush....I got that green...."*

Would be commodities brokers, who are permanently barred from employment at the local exchange, make a "Black Market" in small trades of silver, platinum, diamonds and gold. Single mothers who clean downtown hotel rooms and offices by day, stand on darkly lit street corners at night selling pounds of flesh to repay the Shylocks their high interest payday advance loans. Don't believe the hype, you can find all kinds of "Black Enterprise" around here.

As she got out of the car, the seatbelt bunched her skirt up all the way over her sweaty naked brown ass. The sight of her soft young shiny brown booty unexpectedly made my dick stand up straight and hard as a classroom yardstick. I guess she thought it would fall back down by itself, but it didn't. She finally pulled it down as she walked up the steps to her apartment. Not before anybody that wanted to could get a peak though. *Li'l fast tail Tamika Scott.*

Sometimes you can't tell exactly what you're getting when you pick up one of these girls off the street. If you were to see them the next day in the light, you'd be ashamed of yourself. Although from what I could see from the streetlights, li'l Tamika looked like the streets hadn't been too rough on her.

Her ass was still soft and bouncy and her titties still stood at attention. Her face wasn't cut up as far as I could see and I didn't see too many scratches or sores on her legs either. There didn't seem to be any needle tracks on her arms and her lips weren't dark from sucking on the pipe either. She was still only about twenty-two years old though.

So many of these girls have been on drugs or getting their ass whipped for so long, they don't even notice their good looks left them a long time ago. That is if they ever had any good looks to begin with. They still come out here every night to get that money though. I guess somebody must be fuckin' 'em too, or they wouldn't keep coming out here.

"Have a seat on the sofa."

"Over there????"

"Yeah, over there – sofa" She said sarcastically like I might say to a child in my class who missed seeing something obvious. "You want something to drink????"

"No, I'm good"

"You like my crib????"

"Yeah it's cool"

She went into the kitchen to fix herself a drink. I sat down and tried to get comfortable and have a look around. I must say her place was pretty nice. It was clean and smelled like citrus *Glade*, not piss and greens.

The furniture was about as nice as could be expected for Rent-A-Center furniture. It seemed like she had her own idea of what a nice home should look like, she just hadn't quite made it there yet. The big ass TV, the glass tables and the Oriental fans on the walls were to be expected, but the furniture wasn't too loud or *"Dope Boy Fresh"*. No man lived here.

There were a bunch of pictures of one cute little girl sitting on each end table and one on top of the TV with her hugging the little girl tightly. There wasn't a single posed pictures of the "Baby Daddy", "Mack Daddy", "Sugar Daddy" or "Pimp Daddy" she was waiting for to get out of jail. Not even a shot of their one big night out with a "Baller", at the club posing with money in his hands standing in front of a *Bentley* background. I couldn't help but notice that I didn't see a high school diploma either.

"You sure you don't want something to drink"

"No. I'm straight." It felt like an inside joke as soon as I said it.

""You don't talk much do you???? My mama said to always watch out for them quiet ones. She said y'all were trouble. So what kind of trouble you want to get into tonight????"

"I'm down for whatever." *Yeah I'm down allright.*

"You sure you can handle that?????"

"I know I can"

"Well, I'm gonna finish this *Remy*, then we can take care of *business*."

As she sat in the chair next to the end table, I couldn't help but notice the pictures of the little girl next to her. The innocent looking angel in the pictures looked just like the little girl that used to be in my class. She didn't remember who I was, but I must admit those pictures were fucking with me. I didn't feel bad because I was over here trying to escape my problems by fucking her. I felt bad because fucking and sucking guys like me seemed to be the only thing she had going on in her life, except for her beautiful little girl.

I saw that little girl sitting in front of me. I couldn't help but think about why this girl, who could have been anything if she put her mind to it, ended up being a whore. I asked myself all the usual questions. Was she abused, raped, neglected, unwanted, unloved????…..Maybe the schools failed her. Did her parents fail her? Did the system fail her? Maybe I had failed her. One thing is for sure, somebody had. Were there really no simple answers???? How could I even ask "How did this happen to her????" I already knew how this happened to her.

"I just thought about something. I need to go around the corner and check on my baby right quick. I want to kiss her goodnight before she goes to bed. You don't mind do you???? She's over at my cousin's house. He just stays around the corner. I'll be right back."

"You need me to give you a ride????"

"No it's not a problem. I just need to check on her. Just make yourself comfortable. I'll be right back."

Fuck!!!! I could've given her a ride, brought her ass back home, told her I wasn't feeling it anymore, gave her a little money and then took my stupid ass home. Fuck!!!! What the fuck am I doing here???? I might just get the fuck on while she's gone anyway. Damn!!!! Where did she put her cigarettes????? Fuck!!!! Let me go in here and fix myself a drink. Shit!!!!! I need to piss like a Carolina racehorse. Where is her bathroom???? I'll just write her a note, take a piss, and then get the hell out of here. What the fuck have I gotten myself into????

After I came out of the bathroom I sat back down. I decided to finish my drink and calm down. Then I'd leave. All of a sudden, one of the bedroom doors started opening slowly. My heart was racing. So this is it – the big set up.

In the dimmed lights of the apartment, I couldn't tell whether it was an angel, an imp, a seraphim or a ghost. To my surprise, I saw a confused looking, sweet, blurry-eyed six year old girl walking down the hallway. She walked into the living room and stood in front of the chair where Tamika was sitting just a few minutes ago. She was wearing a lemon yellow cotton nightgown and holding a big book in her little hands. The book had a piece of tablet paper and a pencil stuck between the pages. I had to rub my eyes to make sure I wasn't seeing things.

"Mister, do you know where my Mommy is????"

"No sweetie. She didn't bring you home with her????"

"Damon brought me home earlier."

"Who is Damon? Is that your Daddy????" What kind of question was that????

"No *Day-Day* that's my Cousin. He gave me this note to give to Mommy when she got home. He told me to stay in my room and keep the door closed and not to let anybody in. He said he would come back to check on me. He said Mommy was gone too long and he had to go *take care of some business*. I got scared by myself, so I turned on the nite-light and started reading about *The Princess*. Did *"Day-Day"* tell you to come over and watch me????"

"No he didn't, but I will watch you until your Mommy comes back. Is that okay????"

"Okay. You can read the book to me" She said like an enthusiastic pupil to her favorite teacher.

"Okay. I'll read it to you."

"Let's sit over here in Mommy's chair." She said.

The Light Princess and the Lords of the Underworld
By Lady *Cofitachiqui*

Long ago, when most of the world was filled with darkness and evil, there lived a beautiful Light Princess. The Princess lived in a magnificent mountain palace, in a sunny kingdom by the sea. Everyone was happy there because they were always good to each other and everybody always told the truth. Everyone was happy except for the evil Lords of the Underworld. They never told the truth. Their lies would always come back to haunt them.

The Princess lived with her Mother, the Queen of Kindness and her Father, the King of Compassion. They made sure she had everything she needed. She always had enough to eat and they gave her lots of love and attention. They promised her that they would always take care of her. Everybody always told her that she could accomplish anything she put her mind to, as long as she was good to people and always told the truth.

The Light Princess only wanted to do good, but her evil cousins the Lords of the Underworld were always trying to get her to do bad. When she was younger, The King and Queen were always around to guide her. As she got older, there were times when she had to find ways to resist her Cousin's evil ways on her own.

Her Cousin's would always try to get her to….

"Ke-Ke what are you doing out of bed!?!?!?!? What are you doing sittin' up here with this man???? Where is your Mama????"

"Hey Uncle Damon. We're just reading a story. I think Mommy went to go find you." Her sweet little voice squeaked.

"Oh lord. Well put the book up and go back to bed now. I'll finish reading you the story tomorrow."

"No!!!!" She whined. "I want to finish reading it now. You mess up some of the words, Day-Day. He reads it just like my teacher reads it at school."

"Child, put that Damn book up and go to bed!!!!" Day-day ordered.

"Okay. Goodnight Mister. Thank you for reading me the story. I already know how it ends anyway. Do You????"

"No how does it end sweetie."

"The Princess learns that if you always tell the truth you'll always be happy and if you don't tell the truth bad things will happen. Good night Mister. Good night Uncle Damon."

Damon....*Day-Day...Slick*. Tamika may not remember me, but her Cousin damn sure will. All the faggots in Chicago knew Slick. He could get you anything you wanted, whether you wanted some Ecstasy, young boys, straight men or whatever you were into. Occasionally he would hook one of his lesbian friends up with a couple for a threesome, but mostly he catered to other faggots and their vivid imaginations. He hooked me up the first time with Byron, the guy I was with earlier.

Slick wasn't a pimp, but more like a full service "Favor Broker." By day he was a store manager at a *Harold's Chicken*. It was mostly at night when he got his hustle on though. He catered to Chicago's elite business, political and professional class of sissies. He would hook them up discreetly with the roughneck "Hot Boys" who they legislated against, unjustly prosecuted and wouldn't hire to clean their toilets in their other world. He could understand if you were in the closet, but he didn't believe in being on the "Down Low." That shit really pissed him off. You never wanted to piss Slick off.

I heard somebody say his favorite Aunt had died of AIDS because her pretty boy pimp ass "Old Man" didn't let her know he liked fucking boys too. What the fuck had I gotten myself into???? The more important question was how the fuck was I going to get out of it.

"Now look here Nigga, I don't know exactly what the fuck you think you're doing, but you ain't gonna be doing it no mo' around here tonight. You understand me Nigga????"

"Wait a minute Slick, I can explain….."

"Can we go outside???? The baby don't need to hear this shit. In fact you're gonna take me back to my house. You can bring Tamika back over here, then you gonna take your confused Black ass home. Please Believe."

"What about Lakeisha. You're just gonna leave her here by herself again????"

"What about Lakeisha????" He asked mockingly. ".... Nigga, don't come up in here with that concerned "Hangin' wit' Mr. Cooper, Boston Public, Joe Clark" bullshit .Your faggot ass wasn't concerned about no Lakeisha when you came over here to do whatever you was trying to do. What the fuck are you doing over here????? Look Nigga can we just go now!!!!"

Tracy Perdue-Hampton, Esquire, successful married career woman. Waking up by myself again....while my husband's out doing God knows what to Heaven knows who. I'm starting to get really tired of this shit. Coming home at all hours of the morning smelling like cheap liquor and funk. I don't know if he's at the gay bar or the "Tittie Bar". My Momma told me not to marry him. My Daddy told me not to marry him too. I remember my Sister telling me to remember what Daddy always used to say "What's in the blood has got to come out."

I never saw him with a man, but I used to hear other people talk. We would stay up all night talking. He would always talk about what the "Bros" were doing, but never himself. How many girls this guy was fucking, what this dude made this girl or these girls do. With him it was always how some girl was sweatin' him but he wasn't feelin' her.

We started out as just good friends, but I eventually fell in love with him. I know in his own way he loves me too. I know it sounds crazy, but I really thought that if he was gay I could change him. After we got married, I figured out that wasn't possible. It's time for everybody to stop living this lie now. Starting this morning, we're gonna start telling the truth around here. I guess I'll just watch the news until he drags his ass in here. At least I can take my mind off of it by listening to somebody else's problems.

....Thank you for watching WMAQ Channel 5 News in the A.M. In news overnight, an African-American male identified as Damon Scott has been found dead in a Southside neighborhood that is well known for drugs and prostitution. He was found in a car stabbed multiple times by an unknown assailant. We will bring you more details as they become available. In other news....

"Ke-Ke where is Damon. I went to Auntee's house and he wasn't there. Do you no where he went!!!!????"

"He left with the teacher."

"Who????"

"The man who read the book about the Princess to me. Uncle Damon left you a note. The teacher did to."

"Go get it please. Ooohhh I could kill Damon."

"I put them in my book."

"Well go get it please."

"Mommy can you finish reading me the book."

"It's too late sweetie. I'll finish reading it to you tomorrow."

"Please Mommy. We were about to get to the good part."

"What part is that sweetie????"

"You know the part where the Queen tells the little girl how to be happy."

"It'll all still be the same story when you wake up in the mornin' sweetie."

"You promise Mommy????"

"I promise sweetie."

Vince Vanguard Vainglorious

Vainglorious Press 2007

The Wooing of Maryanne Pureheart

In any triangle of love, there comes a time when one must choose. Love as we all know was made for two. This Christmas Eve was Marryanne Pureheart's time to choose.

Marryanne had two young suitors, Ian Sencere and Truth Lovejoy. They were both fine young men of stud-like breeding and an impeccable sense of style. Dashing was young Ian, bling, bling and all. Truth was a gentleman in the best sense of the word. Marryane was no slouch herself. She was a very beautiful young maiden, with a tight body, an "apple bottom", and a gorgeous grill. She also had a heart of gold - you could say she was all that.

It just so happened late one evening that her two beaus arrived at her crib at the same time. Marryanne was unfaded. She took this as a sign and used the opportunity to announce to her two boos that she was going to make a choice.

"I love you both", She said "but I must make a choice." She continued to spit game at them as she fluttered about the crib"…therefore I have decided that the one who gives me that bomb gift on Christmas Eve will win my heart." They both accepted the challenge and signified their exuberance by a resounding shout of "Word!!!!"

The two young players eagerly set out to find just the right gift to win at this game of love. After several days had passed, the crucial time had finally come. They were summoned to appear before the fair Marryane to present their prize winning booty on call.

She was very excited and could not wait to find out what manner of bling and things the gentleman had purchased with their hard earned cheddar. Ian was well prepared as usual, his gift all wrapped and ready to give. He was confident of his impending victory; fore he knew his present was sure to please. After all he did spend much loochie.

On the other hand, after a considerable amount of thought, Truth had failed to come up with a suitable gift in time. It did not help matters that his pockets were not quite as fat as Ian's. On the way to her house, it so happened that he passed by the neighborhood florist. He went inside and decided to buy a simple dozen of roses.

The two gentlemen arrived once again at the same time to present their fateful gifts. It appeared that Ian was empty handed, but he informed them that his gift was outside. The curious ménage all three, preceded alfresco where wrapped in a red ribbon was a shiny black Bentley Continental GT - a very phat whip indeed. Marryane was quite thrilled and almost overcome with joy. It was now Truth's turn.

He would surely have to be up on his hustle to top Ian's bold display of mad skills. Much to Ian's surprise, Truth's heart did not pump Kool Aid and he stood his ground unvexed. From behind his back he brought forth a white box bound by a much smaller red ribbon, which was of curious size compared to Ian's big package. Marryane pulled out her platinum Tiffany scissors, cut the ribbon and opened the simple box. She gazed upon the beautiful red roses and silently read Ian's heartfelt card. She was genuinely moved to tears. She tucked the note into her Prada bag and wiped away both of their tears with her pastel Versace handkerchief.

She chose Truth.

Ian was outraged. "I am reproached fair lady and I dare say Good Sir I shall demand satisfaction." Ian exclaimed. "I spent a whole lot of time and hard earned scrilla trying to woo you – What's the business baby?!?!?!?!"

To which she replied, "My reason is simple enough Good Sir. In games of love 'tis easy to get got, when all you invest is money and spend a whole lot. In affairs of the heart 'tis quite easy to see – true love always prevails over insincerity."

Remembering the many good times they shared, she stood tiptoed upon her Jimmy Choo's and kissed the heartbroken Ian upon his left cheek. Alas, he knew the streets had spoken. He bowed to both the lady and her champion and disappeared into the cold, dark night. He jumped into his new Bentley and decided to go in search of a late night club where the girls were showing love. As for Marryanne and Truth, they would retire to the boudoir, where they would spend the rest of this eve spreading Christmas cheer.

Vince Vanguard Vainglorious

Vainglorious Press 2006

Traps

My buddy Joe invited me out this fine evening to celebrate his birthday at this "hole in the wall" neighborhood corner bar and grill named CJ's. Joe was a fairly successful real estate broker, but he still had a lifelong fondness for such urban public houses as this one. Despite its reputation for danger and daring do and the scarcity of "marrying types" women to be found inside, you could still find him at CJ's almost every Friday night.

I must admit, an appreciation for such establishments is something we had in common. People call it slumming when "upscale", educated, professional type people hang out in such places where regular "salt of the earth" working class types gather for a drink and some hot wings. Nevertheless, I have always felt just as at home in these types of joints as I am in pillow padded plush soul lounges and velvet roped upscale jazz clubs.

When I was a kid, my Brother and I would spend the weekends with my Dad after the divorce. He would often take us to such a neighborhood place during the daytime to get a "split" or a hamburger and a coke. We'd play the big basketball video game on the wall for hours while he talked to his friends between sips of *Private Stock* and frequent interruptions for quarters.

He would even teach us a thing or two on the pool table in the back before the other grownups started filtering in. After it got dark we would walk back to the apartment without him. This was long before they days where people feared the missing of and messing with of children. We didn't wait up for him, since we always knew he would come back home sometime before we awoke to the smell of sausages, toast and eggs.

Even during the day, the bar and grill would still be full of hardcore neighborhood drunks and various other colorful persons of interest. Many a lost soul would pass away their days at the bar, drowning their sorrows in cheap gin and bittersweet juice. Other local professionals, who serviced the neighborhood's various needs, would conduct their breadwinning enterprises inside the joint astride the red leather stools or in the black Naugahyde padded booths in the back near the pool tables.

The place was no stranger to drama during the day either. From time to time, the owner Mr. Clyde would have to club some cat over the head with a bat for disrespecting his fine "old lady" Miss Peaches with too many off color comments about her big red "titties". Occasionally, women would even "duke it out" if one of them found her "old man" hugged up in the booth with some other broad.

In those days, good kids were cherished by all adults and everybody in the neighborhood knew and looked out for Willie's, handsome, smart, well behaved little boys. So no harm would ever come to us, even in a place like that. As long as we stayed in our place and didn't try to mind grown folks business, everyone made an effort to shield us from the dark side of what went on in the bar.

These were very poor working class people, but that didn't stop my Dad's stumbling drunk friends from rummaging through their pockets to find a quarter each to give us to buy a "Moon Pie" or play another arcade game. Every Friday night I would lay awake in my Dad's bed, wondering what he was up to down there. Many years later, I would find out for myself exactly what took place in those forbidden places, between twilight and dawn.

I arrived at CJ's later than my buddy said he would be there, but after walking around a few times I didn't see him. I didn't see anybody else I wanted to meet either so I decided to leave and come back later. It was relatively early still, so I figured I'd go hunting at a few other places nearby.

Another good thing about these types of fine establishments found on the "Westside" is that they somehow managed to serve my favorite Tanqueray and cranberry juice cocktails for $2 each. The clubs on the other side of town charged three or four times more for the same thing. This made such places very convenient for having a couple drinks before and after hitting the well-heeled nightspots Uptown or the exposed brick wall bohemian haunts Downtown. Also, the women that frequented these lively watering holes tended to live very close by, which made it somewhat easier - to get to know them better.

After making a few stops around town, I was disappointed that I didn't find anybody else I wanted to make friends with. I decided that I might as well head back over to CJ's to look for Joe again. I made my way inside and stopped just a few feet from the front door. I figured that if I didn't see my friend I could easily just walk right back out. I didn't see him right away. I also could see that not too many new women had found their way inside the club since I was there before.

As I was looking around nonchalantly for my buddy, I glanced at this woman walking in my direction. She looked as if she was about to leave. As she got closer though, I could see she wasn't leaving. She was headed straight towards me. She stopped right in front of me and touched me on the arm. With a big longingly shy smile on her face, she looked up at me and said "I was hoping you'd come back."

She told me her name was Faye and this was her first time at CJ's in years. I was pretty sure I'd never met her before, but I still felt a little uneasy. In those days it would not be beyond the realm of possibilities for me to get to know somebody very well and not remember what they looked like, let alone remember their name. As we continued to talk though, I decided that if there was going to be some drama it would have happened by now, so I started to feel a little more at ease.

I must admit I was a little flattered, but the unexpected attention still seemed kind of strange. When I was there the first time I didn't notice her at all. I thought I had checked out everything in the club. Despite the opportunity that presented itself, I continued to look for Joe as we talked. Finally, I spotted him sitting in the corner with some other guys. I politely told her I saw the guys I was here to meet, so I had to cut our conversation short. I said it was nice to meet her and I would say bye before I left.

I made my way through the crowd of Friday night just got paid neighborhood revelers, greeted my boy with a "Soul Brother's Birthday hug", gave him some dap and wished him a Happy Birthday. "Derek!!!! What's up boy???? Good to see you. Get you something to drink" he said as the ember glowed brightly from the Black and Mild cigar that dangled from his lips.

He and the rest of his crew hadn't been there long, but they had managed in a short time to build up a very nice collection of empty 40 ounce "*OE*" bottles, plastic cups and a mountain of *Newport* butts in a gold metal ashtray. Somebody handed me a yellow 16 ounce plastic cup right away. I guess they thought I had some catching up to do. Little did they know I was pretty far ahead.

Before long, I shared with them the story of what happened when I walked inside the club. I pointed out the young lady sitting at the bar. She'd been sitting there all night long, talking to the female bartender. Now I must admit, she wasn't that graciously graced in the "grill", but she did have a very nice little petite body with a tight little ass. Regardless of her shortcomings in the visage, she looked good enough for them to give me their unanimous late night ghetto "brew crew" seal of approval. I guess that was all the encouragement I needed.

Besides, I was really drunk now and a little horny, so it didn't take much to set the wheels of lust in motion. They continued to encourage me with their various ghetto colloquialisms that all basically translated into "Dog, I'd hit that ass if I was you." So after a little while longer, I bid them all a farewell and a good night and proceeded to the bar to do what I "had" to do.

As soon as I walked over, she told me she was glad I came back because she was about to leave. She introduced me to the bartender Gayle, who worked there nights, but who she knew from working their day job together. We said goodnight to her friend and proceeded out the door to her car.

We talked for a while as we leaned against her ride. After we exchanged phone numbers, I promised her we'd see each other again. I really wasn't intending to see her again, so I decided to get in her car on the passenger's side with the intention of closing this little chapter tonight.

Even though I took a bit of a chance, she found my quasi-vulgar attention and hyper drunken intrusion into her personal *ridespace* quite charming and curiously flattering. Within a few minutes of telling several time tested lies, I leaned forward and gave her a lethal kiss on her neck. In no time we were fogging up her windows kissing and groping each other like Joanie and Chachi in the parking lot of *Arnold's Drive In*.

There is something that really turns me on when I look at ladies' wide open legs when she's sitting in the driver's seat of a car. Especially when they're driving some really fast fly flashy shit. The thought of this little 5'2" chick with her nice little ass handling this big Mustang Boss 5.0 made my dick hard as Chinese arithmetic. I couldn't help but reach up under her skirt and stick my finger up into her tight, hot little pussy.

In no time at all, one of my thick fingers stroking back and forth inside of her caused her to flow as freely as one of the beer taps at Sam Malone's Boston bar. She was so wet now that I was able to push in another finger. I wanted to get her used to the thickness of the new stick she would soon be driving. Then I took her left hand off the top of mine and I placed it on my zipper. We unzipped it together and she reached inside my jeans and cupped her small hand under my balls. She started stroking them like they were precious black pearls.

I was too drunk to remember where I was or even who I was with now and too hyped up and horny to care. I was lost in the oblivion of this delightfully unexpected chance encounter. After a few minutes though, it did dawn on her that we weren't parked very far from the front door of the spot.

Apparently we had been providing light entertainment for all of the other patrons who were making their way to their cars after leaving the club. I really didn't give a fuck, but she was a little embarrassed. I would never see any of these people in my "real" life. Anyway, we stopped and got our shit together.

I got out of the car and came around to her side, then I leaned inside her window and kissed her softly on the cheek. I promised that I'd see her tomorrow. Of course I had to see her again now. It would be the only "gentlemanly" thing to do.

As soon as I walked into good old CJ's Saturday night, I saw a sweet looking lady sitting at the bar whose face I vaguely remembered. She waved at me from across the nearly empty club. I started walking towards the bar since – I guess that must be her. She introduced me to her friend again, as if she was the one who was too drunk to remember me. We sat at the bar and made awkward small talk like we were on a blind date. I ordered a couple of Tanqueray and cranberries as we continued to chat. I noticed her and the bartendress kept smiling and giggling at each other and they continued to trade certain gestures and head nods while we talked.

Eventually, she worked up the nerve to translate their naughty little sign language to me. She told me that her friend lived close by and we could go to her house if I liked. "We could get to know each other a little better in private" is how she coyly stated it. I'm not sure why they thought I needed to be convinced.

We walked inside of her girlfriend's little rented West End house, but I don't think Faye had ever been there before. She didn't seem to know which bedroom belonged to Gayle. Eventually, we decided on the room with the clean white sheet covered mattress, lying on the floor with no box springs or frame. I was so excited. This shit was gonna be raw. I soon realized that she had something very different in mind.

As we began to undress each other, I was in a bit of a rush. I started to unzip her jeans so I could finally go to work on that little heart shaped ass, but she held both my hands firmly with a surprising amount of strength and gently guided them down to my sides. As she unbuttoned my shirt, she kissed me softly across the chest from top to bottom. The pace suddenly slowed.

We began to exchange tender sensual embraces and deep penetrating soul melting kisses as we peeled away each other's clothes. Once there were no more layers to uncover or places to discover, I cradled her in my arms and guided her down gently to the mattress. We twisted and tangled into an indistinguishable heap as we writhed and slithered into a corporeal knot. After exploring each others bodies from all angles with tender touches and unrestricted tongues, we were now face to face once again.

She stared deeply into my eyes as if she'd found something she had lost or at least something she was searching for, but never had. Then she wrapped her legs around my hips and dug her fingernails into my shoulders like a cat stuck in a tree. It felt as if she was holding on to a breaking branch for dear life. I arched my back like I was the King of the jungle and thrust my scepter deep into her enchanted Garden of Eden. Her river flowed endlessly like the Nile. We spent what seemed like an eternity on this sacred nocturnal safari, exploring every emotion and motion that was humanly possible, upon this clean white sheeted oasis.

We finally came to rest and lay motionless in the dark. As we lay still on this strange mattress that was now baptized in perfume, alcohol, sweat and tears, the silence finally broke as she began to speak. She wanted to tell me about herself and her life and why she was out last night at CJ's. I tried at first to derail her groove by talking about how good the pussy was and asking her how many times she came. She answered my question, but continued to talk about herself, her life and why she was at CJ's last night. I didn't really want to get into anything this heavy, but I couldn't ignore that what we had just shared went well beyond casual sex.

Faye told me that she had gotten to know her friend the bartender at CJ's because she worked in some other capacity at the AIDS hospice where she was a nurse. She had already told me about her job when we talked on the phone earlier today. I found it truly fascinating. I didn't even know such places existed and was shocked to know one existed in a city like Houston. I was even more shocked at how many patients in those early days of the epidemic she said she was responsible for taking care of. Even though I wasn't looking for love off in the "juke joint" I knew she was different from the other girls up in CJ's last night. I realized that it took a very sweet, compassionate, loving – a special person to do that kind of work. Like I said though, I wasn't looking to meet my soul mate at the hole in the wall.

Then she told me that her friends from work insisted that she needed to get out and meet somebody "new". Apparently all she did was work, come home from work and take care of her kids after taking care of dying people all day, every day. Then she would wait for her husband to get home so he could beat her ass every night. Yes, she was married and I already knew that too.

She told me his name, but I blocked it out as soon as she said it. She met him in college, back when she was a cheerleader and he was a glorious strapping jock. Now she was a nurse with a job she loved and kids she adored. He was a washed up athlete who hated being married and couldn't find any other work except being a security guard. His only qualifications for the job were the ability to be big and upright for eight hours. She said that the meaningless life he led made him bitter and cruel. Somehow rather than take refuge in her love, he felt it necessary to whip her ass to the point that she was too sore to go to work every day, but she still did.

One night, somehow she found out he was fucking around with another woman. He certainly hadn't been fucking her in quite a long time, so she was a little pissed. Even though she hated it when they "made love" he was still her husband.

She decided to confront him about it. She expected that he would show some remorse and ask forgiveness for going out fucking some trick while she was at work all day making money to take care of the family. She believed that he must still love her enough to give her that much respect.

Instead she says that he kicked her ass from one room to the other until she finally ended up lying on the ground in the kitchen unable to move. Then he stumped on her back and left her lying in the middle of the floor motionless as he walked out the door to go find his refuge some place else. Despite her physical pain and her spiritual desolation, she managed to pick herself up off the ground and clean up the house and herself. She had no choice - the kids would be home from school soon. I was ready to kick this motherfucker's ass.

I asked her why didn't he just leave and of course she said that he told her that he didn't want anybody else to have her or any other man raising his kids. Even though I was mad as hell, I remembered momentarily that I had been fucking this man's wife who barely knew me for the better part of the night while her kids were

God knows where. I decided that maybe I should gather a few more details. She continued to tell me about her years of abuse and frankly, it was almost more than I could stand.

Despite the small fact that I might be wrong for fucking this man's wife, I was still sincerely motivated to whip his Black ass. I asked her, where was he right now while she was out all night with me. Much to my surprise, she told me that he was up the street working security at Grogan's Groceries, a few minutes away from the club.

I didn't know what to think now. Was she telling me the truth about her situation???? Was she just looking for somebody to set him up???? Was she just plain old crazy???? I decided that she must be telling the truth because no woman would make up a story like that. I don't know if I was just stupefied by a powerful case of post pussy machismo or overcome by a turn of bad judgment in the name of neo-soul chivalry but, I was like "Okay cool, I'll go whip his ass for you right now." After about another hour or so of further "encouragement"….we got dressed and headed up to the parking lot of Grogan's.

She parked on the other side of the lot from where he was standing. There was more than one "Top Flight" security officer standing out front so I confirmed which one he was. She pointed out her husband as the fairly large one leaning against the rail on the side street end of the building, with his back foot up on the rail. She asked me what I was going to do???? Since he was no bigger than any other dude I had ever scrapped with – I told her, "I'm gonna go whip his ass like I said."

As I got out of the car though, I decided that I still couldn't just walk up to this dude on her word and just start going upside his head. So I got the bright idea that I would walk through the store on the end where the car was parked and come out on his side. Then I would start a casual conversation with him. I'd figure out a way to tell him what I knew and then I'd whip his ass. Wait does that make sense????

Sure enough I came out of the automatic doors and walked right in front of him. Suddenly something dawned on me though. It occurred to me that I might lose the advantage of my moral outrage if he found out so abruptly that I had just finished fucking his wife in the ass a few minutes ago. How could I tell him that I knew his wife because I had spent the last three or four hours since he started his shift, with the mother of his children's legs wrapped around my waist. So I decided I would ask him for some directions first.

"Brother uh, do you know how to get to Chickamauga Avenue???? I asked. He didn't look at all like what I was expecting.

To my surprise, this brute, this bully, this ogre, this coward walked over to me and put his hand on my shoulder so he could kindly point me towards the street. I thought he was about to point at his wife's car and ask me "Nigga didn't I just see you get out of that car over there????"

Instead this despicable beast gave me the most detailed, clear and thorough directions I had ever received in my life. He seemed to take pride in his work even though this wasn't really even part of his job. Complete with pointing and hand gestures, this thoughtful "Brother" seemed to be genuinely concerned that I make it safely where I was going. I was stunned and not sure what to do next.

I had just learned this man's entire pitiful life story over the last few hours. Even though it was almost 4am and he was standing outside in the cold at a job he hated and waiting desperately 'til 7am so he could go home to his other miserable existence, he managed to muster the concern it took to give a stranger thorough directions to some place that I had no intention of even going to. He seemed somehow to want to prove to me that he was useful, by showing me how much pride he took in doing his work. Where was the monster I was looking for????

On the other hand, I was standing in front of him with the scent of his wife's yoni on my shirt and still feeling moist places on my body from her yet to dry feminine essences. Suddenly, I had the strange feeling that his wife was sitting in the car praying that I take care of a problem for her that the cause and true nature of which may not be quite what I was led to believe. It was at that moment that I thanked him and walked back towards his wife's car. He in turned returned to his time passing conversation with his colleague. When I got to the car, she asked me what happened. I told her I just wanted to size him up – for next time.

I wish that I could tell you that was the last time I saw her, but it wasn't. As we continued to see each other I learned that her stories were indeed true, but there was some gray. I wish I could tell you I eventually took care of her problem for her, but I didn't. As I came to know her better, I realized that nothing justified his abuse, but I also learned that he had a story of his own. I wish I could tell you that I feel bad now about fucking that man's wife, but I don't. I learned that night that life can be complicated and sometimes very cruel. Not everybody gets the love or the life that they want or need. I learned that sometimes, for some people, stealing a few tender moments with a stranger in a dark strange room is as good as life ever gets.

Vince Vanguard Vainglorious

Vainglorious Press 2006

Causeway

This li'l show in Savannah was just what me and Tiffany needed. We needed to get away before we got deep into this wedding planning shit. We finally set a date for the wedding; September 14th is the big day. We got about two months to do the damn thang right.

Besides we were both getting pretty sick of all the groupies and homies following me around back at home. I'm really hot right now. My new album just went platinum so I can't go nowhere in the "H" without somebody sweatin' me. I ain't as big in Georgia yet, like back home in Houston. Savannah ain't Atlanta either so I figure we can kick back and relax a little bit here.

"Baby ain't you got family down this way????" I ask her, trying to see if she's still awake.

"Yeah baby, in Charleston – that's in South Carolina though" I can tell I caught her right before she was about knocked out.

"Charleston still in South Carolina???? You sho' is edumacated" I reply sarcastically.

"Boy stop. Where we at anyway????" She says as she stretches out her slender body and yawns.

"I thank we in some li'l town called Pooler, Georgia. That's what the sign back there said. Sound like some real country shit don't it???? Maybe you can put some of that smartness to work and see where we at on the map????"

"You ain't lyin'. Let me find it."

She's in her second year of law school at Rice now. I really can't believe she's still fuckin' wit' a thug ass nigga like me. Well ex-thug I should say, but I owe most of that to her.

Me and Tiff went to high school together, but didn't start dating until a few years after we graduated. I was straight thugged out from the Fifth Ward. Still is really – gotta be in this business. She was one of them "bougie" babes whose daddy had a "good job" inspectin' buildings for the city or some shit.

Our paths never really crossed back then, since I'm from the other side of the tracks as they say. I met her at our homecoming football game when I came back to show off all the "Bling" I bought from the first album. That platinum around my neck was everything I had in the world, but nobody knew it. I came at her wit' that thug shit at first, but she wasn't hearing none of it. I could tell she was gone check any disrespect that came out of my mouth real quick. I knew right away that she could see it was mo' to me than some beats, rhymes and a gold grill.

"Baby if we in Pooler that ain't that far from Savannah, if we goin' the right way. We goin' the right way - right????"

"Shit if we is lost it's yo' fault. How the navigator gone fall asleep????"

"Stop playin' boy" She says as she punches me in the shoulder.

As she lands her little love blow to my arm, my other hand slips off the wheel as we hit a bump. I run off the road and the passenger side mirror hits a mile per hour sign. As I look over to make sure it didn't fly off and hit Tiff, I roll into a ditch. We look at each other in disbelief.

I can tell she is scared because of what just happened and because she made me wreck this *Beemer* I just bought last week. I ain't trippin' on that though, since finally I can afford not to be "ridin' dirty." What I am trippin' on is that I ain't got the number for AAA on me.

"Damn girl, you hit harder than when yo' Mama used to box." I say which makes her crack a little nervous smile. "You allright Boo????"

"I'm sorry Baby" she says as she unclips her seatbelt and opens the door. "Yeah, I'm fine."

"Its cool. Anyway – I've got great news. I just saved a bunch of money on my car insurance by switching to Geico." I say as I whip out the imaginary card like I'm doing a commercial.

This gets a full, but short lived laugh out of her. We have a little inside joke about me doing an insurance commercial after all my years of riding around without any. Besides, after everything she had done for me I was more concerned about her than I was my "whip".

When me and Tiff got together she opened up a whole new world to me. She was my eyes and ears in this "Rap Game". She made sure I got what was mine and that I always knew what I was getting myself into. So no matter what I might spit on one of these records or say on the stage, I'm gone always take care of my baby first.

She unclips my seatbelt as I open my door. She gets out and comes around to look at me to see if I'm allright. As we lean against the driver's side door and try to figure out what we're gonna do next, I reach under the seat and pull out a pack of *Newport*s I had been hiding. I reach back into the car to get the lighter.

"I thought you was gone quit" She says scolding me, but in the tone of somebody who just wrecked a nigga's new car.

"I was "shawty", but this some "scressful" shit I say with the smile of somebody still trying to avoid a fight with his woman about quittin' smokin'.

"Anyway where the fuck are we????" She asks.

"Pooler, Georgia, ain't that what you said????"

Now when you are a young Black couple ridin' in a BMW 750 that's crashed on the side of the road after Ten o'clock at night in the "Deep South", the question "Where the fuck are we????" takes on many meanings. The obvious answer though right now is that we definitely ain't in a major city, since not one car has passed by since this shit happened. Now other possible meanings of the question are - *Is this the White side or the Black side of town???? Are there any Black people in this town at all???? Is it a Black town full of thugged out gangsters who gone rob us???? Is it a honky tonk town full of rednecks who gone lynch us???? Do they have a Klan chapter in this town???? Do they have an NAACP chapter in this town????* Basically, when you're a rich and famous "Dirty South" rapper wit' a pretty girl, broke down on the side of the road, in a big body *Beemer,* in the middle of the country, you still can't be sure whether you gone have to sign autographs or get yo' ass lynched.

"Gimme a cigarette." She says. I just turn my head and look at her like she's crazy.

Over the horizon, we see a "Heavy Chevy" with a red candy chrome paint job coming our way. It looks like we must be in the hood. *Thank you Jesus.* As the car gets closer we start to feel even better as we can hear *Field Mob* boomin' crisp out of the Alpines. We're both so happy we almost giggle. As the car gets closer, we see two big White boys gettin' "Crunk" to the beat in the front seat and a li'l Black girl wearing a Shannon Sharpe, Savannah State University throwback jersey sittin' in the middle of the back seat. They fly buy us and don't stop.

As the car "hauls ass", I can see the girl still looking at us through the back window. About two minutes later, another car is approaching from the same direction. Whether it was gonna be *Bo and Luke Duke* or the *Ying Yang Twinz* we couldn't tell.

"Hey baby, maybe you oughta do some of that old time movie shit and stick yo' leg out in the road. Ah-oooga - Ah-ooooga!!!!" I say laughing.

"You shittin' me. Maybe you oughta call one of them groupies from back home to come up here and have her do it." She's not feelin'me right now.

Now half of that was irritation about the situation. The other half was her way of finishing an earlier conversation about a particular hoochie ass stripper who she's seen hangin' around the group more than usual lately. I told her that girl was comin' around to see my DJ Nate, but she just brought it up again to see what I'd say. I used to have a li'l problem saying no to them ho's in the early days, but now it really don't fade me. Since me and Tiff been engaged, I done turned down mo' ass than a used donkey salesman.

"Girl stop playin'. Anyway I don't care if it's the Grand Puba of the Klan or yo' cripple ass Auntee who dance at *Foxxy's. W*e need to get this ride. "I say as I walk to the edge of the road and start waving my arms.

Another girl dressed like the girl in the back of the other car pulls over in an old beat up Honda Prelude. I only got a glimpse of the other girl, but I can see this girl has on the same jersey on top but is only wearing a bikini bottom. I mean she was really wearing it too.

"Y'all allright" she asks.

Now her voice is a little different than even what I'm used to back in Houston – this girl is country. Even in the shadows of the darkness inside of her car, I can also see that she's got an ass on her like a Georgia mule on 'er too. I can smell the scent of not quite completely aired out "Bubba Kush" comin' out the window, mixed in with all of the stale *Newport* butts in the ashtray, spilled Colt 45 on the passenger seat and remixed with a little bit of *Tommy Bahama* perfume. This girl is "'Bout it 'Bout it"

The craziest shit though is what I hear as I'm leaning into the car to talk to her. I can faintly hear the commercial for my show on the radio. Just as I was about to start talking, Tiff stepped in to start the negotiations for a ride.

"Excuse me Miss, My name is Tiffany…." She says as she nudges in next to me and sticks her handshaking hand in li'l shawty's dank smelling car "….and this is my fiancé Bernard. We had a little accident and we were wondering if you could give us a ride to the city????"

"My name Tiffani too, but I spell it wit' two I's. What town y'all goin' to????" She asks in a Southern drawl like her tongue had been dipped in Alaga syrup "Y'all must be goin' ta Brunswick????

"N'all shawty…." I speak up out of habit and because I can tell I speak her language"….we tryin' to get to Savannah."

"Ya'll done already passed Savannah, Boo. This Hinesville. I can give y'all a ride back to Savannah, but I gotta go handle some business first if that's a'ight wit y'all???? Uh, is that yo' car there Boo-Boo???? I wouldn't leave it out here too long. So y'all ridin' wit me or what????"

There was no way to tell if or when somebody else was gonna come along so we decided to ride with her. Tiffany sat up front with her and I got in the back after I moved all the baby toys, teddy bears and empty *Happy Meal* boxes out of the way. The only question on my mind though was what the fuck kinda business was she going to handle dressed like that. It didn't take long to get the answer though.

"I dance." She said with the pride little girls have when they tell their Mama they got picked for the pep squad. "I gotta go up to Fort Stewart and do a li'l "Special" for the groom at this li'l country ass bachelor party these white boys havin'" "Can y'all smell that????" She asks referring to nothing in particular. I'm not sure if she means the Newports, the Kush, the Tommy or the hint of old spoiled baby formula wasted in the back, but I answer anyway.

"N'all you straight Shawty. What smell????" I could see that Tiff cocked her head a little so I could see her impish smile.

"Oh nuttin' nuttin'. Jus a li'l sum sum." Tiffani spelled with two I's says.

"You good "Shawty". Do you." I say.

"So what y'all doin' all the way out here????? That's a pretty car you to'e up back there. You play for the Falcons or somethin'????"

"N'all we just on a li'l road trip visitin' fam' that's all."

I'm not sure how much farther we have to go, but I know I don't want to answer all these damn questions all the way there. As I'm about to ask her to turn up the radio though, Tiff decides to reverse the twenty questions game on her.

"So how long you been dancing????" She asks like a cool ghetto high school guidance counselor.

"Bout two years comin' up soon. I go to school for paralegal too, but a Bitch gotta do what she gotta do. You know????."

After the "B" word got tossed out there, I could tell Tiff was a little tripped out and wanted to get into some deep respect yo' self shit or get all I am woman hear me roar on her ass. She was smart enough to know that we didn't know where the fuck we were and we were in her funky ass car that she was sweet enough to give us a ride in. Personally, I thought the shit was kind of funny.

You got two females named Tiffany/Tiffani stuck in this situation wit' my Black ass. One is a stripper and one hate strippers. They both in school trying to do the best they can. Right now though, the one wit' everything going for her, need a ride from a country ass, would-be paralegal stripper, a lot more than we need a future lawyer. Like they say, it takes all kinds. Please believe.

Sometime I thank its good for Tiffany to see that everybody else ain't had it easy like she did. The fact of the matter was that my Tiff really didn't know nothin' about "What a "Bitch gotta do." Her folks paid for college and she never went without when we was in high school either. If you wanna be real about it, I love my girl but I know a lot more girls like the other Tif.

I do understand what she goin' through. I hope she make it too. It's really fucked up that she gotta dance and shit. You know some nigga probably left her wit them babies, but that's just part of the struggle. Anyway, I still gotta make sure my girl don't try to get all Oprah on her ass 'cus we still don't know where the fuck we at. I ain't tryin' to be walkin' around lost out in this *Mississippi Burning* lookin' town. That's why I gotta make sure nobody say nothin' too stupid.

"My girl she in law school too." I say trying to keep everybody mellow.

"I'm in paralegal school, law school that ain't the same thang honey." Ghetto Tiffani with an I on the end says to me. I guess she told my Black ass.

"Anyway girl, where y'all from????" Tiffani two I's says.

"Houston, that's in Texas." Tiffany with a Y on the end says trying not to laugh at how "li'l Shawty" just busted me out.

After that Tiffani with an I doesn't say anything but turns up the radio for her own behavior modification. I guess she had her fair share of people laughing at her expense and thinking she was stupid. She knew from experience when to let shit die, before some shit got started. I guess she didn't want us two "Bougie", Black, "Beemer" drivin' Negroes to keep her from doing something nice for somebody today.

"….**K-K-K- Krunkfest** 2006 featuring all the way from the "H-Town" *5th **Ward B-B-B-Burner…**" Blared from the Kenwood door speakers. I'm pretty sure shawty put two and two together by now, but she didn't say another word.

We start to pass a whole bunch of military looking shit so I guess this was Fort Stewart. I think my uncle kicked it down here for a minute when he was in the service. There still aren't many cars on the road, but we pull up to a little beige house with about twenty cars parked in the driveway and all over the front lawn.

There are a couple guys hanging outside drinking beer but most everybody else is inside. It seems like they all have the same haircut and they're all "Cock Diesel Swole". I guess they're Marines or SEALS or some shit. I'm thinking maybe we made a mistake since we have no idea how long she was gonna be in there.

"Y'all comin' in or y'all gone stay in the car. I just do my li'l show and make sure "My Girls" okay then I can get the fuck on." She says.

I believe Tiff wanted to stay in the car, but I wasn't going to be able to smell them Newport butts much longer without wanting to smoke one myself. I knew Tiffany just figured I wanted to go in and see them ho's dance. I was curious to know what this "Special" shit was though.

To my surprise, my Tiff says. "We'll be right in, Sweetie"

As we got out of the car, she turned to me and reminded me that I better just sit my ass down and wait for our ride. Like I said, I used to have a little problem with this stripper attention when I first got a li'l change in my pocket. Being with Tiff made me realize how fucked up it was to want somebody to want you or to want somebody just for the money.

I know dudes like to call women "Gold Diggas" and shit, but the truth is that a lot of niggas get a rush out of women wanting them for their money. Besides the way I figured, if all I wanted from them was some ass, it whatn't nothing wrong with them just wanting my money. I

didn't have shit comin' up, so I wanted to let people know I had money now and didn't mind

watching folks treat me good to try to get it. After I finally met a woman who let me know she

cared about me and not the money, it made me a whole different person.

Don't get it twisted though, Tiff knew her fair share of broke thugs comin' up too, but

she didn't give them no play. She wouldn't have looked at me twice if I was broke either. It was

the fact that I made something out of myself that she liked. It wasn't just the money.

As we walked in the door of the little house, we could see that they were definitely all

military and all White except a few dudes that looked Pilipino or Mexican or somethin'. There

were three girls already dancing and the guys were either watching, standing around talking shit,

or watching the Black on White "Fuck Flick" that was on the big screen. I could see that off in

the corner the li'l cute girl who was riding with the two White boys was off in the cut dancin' for

them, plus two other big White boys. As soon as our driver walked through the door though, the

crowd let out a roar that was a smaller version of what I was used to hearing." I guess it's true

what "Sly" used to sang on my Mama's record – "Everybody is a Star."

"Tiff!!!" "Tiff!!!!" "Tiff!!!!' "Tiff!!!!"

"Hey y'all" she replied. "Everybody having a good time????" She turns to us and whispers

"Y'all make yourself comfortable. I'm gone get this little money then we can leave."

I looked around and decided that we should sit on an empty couch that had been pushed over in the corner in case there was a need for a makeshift private dancer VIP room, in this li'l off-base government soldier's quarters. Tiff sits on the end and I sit in the middle. These boys must have been headed to or just got back from Iraq or somewhere 'cus they was partying like their lives depended on it.

To be honest with you they must have watched a bunch of *Li'l Jon* videos or something 'cus they had this makeshift "Shaky Booty" club hooked up just right. It looked and sounded like we was inside the *Body Tap* down in the ATL. After about 15 minutes of regular dancin', Tif (not my Tiff) announced that she was 'bout to do her thing.

They had already collected the money for her to do whatever this "Special" shit was she does. Everybody got in position to watch the much anticipated show. I felt a big body plunk down on the other cushion of the sofa. I looked to my left and saw one of the biggest of all the big "Rambos" sit next to me. As she made her entrance out of one of the bedrooms, she pointed to the DJ and on cue "Kushin' for the Pushin'" the new hit song *by 5th Ward Burner* came blasting out of the JBLs louder than I'd ever heard it before.

"....*We be smokin' that 'dro pushin' up on these ho's*...." Then all in unison thirty three of the biggest, most clean cut, White boys I had ever seen in my life shouted at the top of their lungs.

*"....**Nigger** what my **Nigger**, I got the Kushin' for the Pushin' for these Stankin' Ass Ho's!!!!!!!!!!! Ride on Nigga!!!! Ride on. Ride on Bitch!!!! Ride on...."*

I ain't gone lie to you, at the same time I was amazed these white boys knew my music; I had never in my life thought about hearing and seeing any shit like this. I wrote this shit, I put it out there, but it never occurred to me that a bunch of country ass White boys would ever be screamin' the word **Nigger** at the top of their lungs, while a Black sister slithered butt ass naked on a dirty floor trying to earn some money to go to school and feed her babies. Was it like old girl said earlier, when I made this was I just doing "What I had to do????"

I grabbed my girl by the hand to step outside. As we were about to leave, I could see that some of the boys were taking the other li'l girl into one of the bedrooms. Tiffani was about to do the trick with a 40 ounce beer bottle, a *Zippo* lighter and a big ass bong that everybody was waiting for her to do all night. My song was the background music for this whole wild ass scene.

"Let's wait outside." I say as I lift Tiff off the couch by her hand and walk out the door.

Tiff gets back into the passenger seat while I lean against the car and smoke a Newport. Two of the guys are still standing outside drinking. I guess they objected to the quality of entertainment inside.

"....Shiiiitt, you wouldn't catch me dead 'round them Motherfuckers at that concert. Them **Niggers** is stupid...."

We really need to go now. I tell Tiff to stay put while I go back in to see how long old girl is gonna be. As I walk inside I see her all up in this big dude's chest screaming and hollerin' about her money.

"I ain't going for this shit again!!!! Now where's the rest of my money!!!!" She screams.

"Hold up **Bitch**, who you screamin' at???? You know me." One of the big White boys from the car says to her.

"Wait a minute podner" I say as I rush over and step in between them. "You got one mo' time to call this woman a **Bitch.** I'll be damn if I'm gone let you get buck up in here." I was dead ass serious, but I couldn't help thinking about how many times I had called this same girl a **Bitch** on and off my records. Matter of fact, that was the reason these dudes thought it was okay to do it too."

The dude chimes back at me in a different kind of Southern drawl that definitely ain't Houston either, "Who the fuck is you Brother???? You her pimp or somethin'????

"N'all podner I ain't no Pimp, but y'all ain't gonna disrespect this female no mo' either."

"Still though, who is ya???? I know you ain't invited. What the hell is you doin' here????"

"Look ponder, My name is ….."

Before I could answer, I hear a voice out of one of the corners yell "Yo!!!! That's 5th Ward Burner!!!! Yo, I got his new CD out in the car."

Big boy responds. "No shit. My bad, "My Nigga". I didn't know. My bad."

"My Nigga" What the hell is going on here???? Just as I'm about to beat the brakes off of this fool for calling me a nigga, I hear the front door slam and Tiffany yells "Bernard!!!! Bernard!!!! I don't give a damn if we gotta walk, but we need to raise the fuck up out of here!!!! Now!!!!"

I rush over to see what the problem is and she tells me that the two drunk soldiers outside came over to the car thinking she was one of the other strippers and was offering her a bunch of money to do a bunch of foul shit. I turn to the other Tiffani to beg her to take us back to Savannah before I end up in jail.

"Look here Nigga, I ain't going no where until these motherfuckers give me the rest of my money." After everything she had done down on that dirty floor, she then added without missing a beat "These motherfuckers are gonna respect me!!!!" As the white boy peeled off a bunch of "Ben Franks" and handed them to her, I couldn't decide if I was still going to whup ole boy's ass now, after ole girl had just called me a Nigga too. I didn't have long to think about it though.

"You still want a piece of me homey???? I paid yo girl and I ain't got no beef wit'chu." He said with all of the confidence of a man who was obviously strapped or had a big "posse". "Shit, I bet some of these boys probably want your autograph." He said.

Tiffany's still standing by the door though and she yell's at us both "Can we please get the fuck out of here????? Ain't none of this shit gone change tonight!!!!"

As we leave out of the house and get in the car, for some reason I thought about the other girls still in there. I couldn't help but wonder if they were gonna be allright after everything that just went down. Tiffani lit a Newport and asked me if I wanted one. I said yes and reached over the seat to take it from her hand. I didn't even look at Tiff since she probably could use one too if she smoked. I took a deep puff as she put the car in reverse.

"Yo homegirls gone be allright????" I ask.

"They'll be allright" she says "They know how to handle their business. Anyway we dance for them Niggers all the time and they always pullin' that same ole shit."

As we head back toward Savannah, I'm having a hard time wit' all this shit and Tiffany with a Y on the end ain't saying a damn thang.

I can see my car just over the hill still sitting in the ditch but a wrecker is approaching from the other direction. A Chatham County deputy's cruiser is already parked in front of the car. Tiffani pulls over so I can get out to talk to the deputy. The deputy is older than the soldier boys back at the party, but he looks just like one of them.

"Is this your car sir????" He asks as he surveys the situation. "Larry there'll getcha outta that ditch, but it's gonna cost you this time of night. You go*t AAA* sir????" He asks with what seems like genuine concern. "Y'all ain't from around here are you???? I see you got Texas plates."

Even with all of the "Sirs" flowing out of his mouth, I'm still waiting for him to start some stupid shit too, but apparently his hood is in the cleaners tonight. "No were just passing through." I respond politely.

"Well sir, if you're okay here, I'm gonna head on down the road. My son's having a bachelor party down in Hinesville. I'm gonna stop down there and make sure they ain't raising too much hell. You and your friends enjoy the rest of your evening." He says as he gets back into the cruiser.

I watched Larry the wrecker guy hook up the car. I couldn't believe how careful he was. I still couldn't help but wonder if those other girls back at the party were okay. I know I wasn't. I walk over to the wrecker to find out from Larry what we need to do next.

"Now y'all can either ride with me or you can follow me in your friend's car." He says. "If you ride with me though, I got a li'l stop I need to make. I gotta li'l business I need to take care of. It won't take me no time though. No time at all."

Vince Vanguard Vainglorious
Vainglorious Press 2006

The Murder of Tupac Shakur Considered as an Illegal Street Race

Mike Tyson waved the Green Flag

The pre-race entertainment began with a championship boxing match, rather than the usual parade of luxurious motorcars and modeling of race attire. The fight ended uneventfully, as the erstwhile champ was felled by a rap on the head from an iron mike.

Everyone's attention would now turn to the true main event. The arrival of the undisputed King of the illegal street racing circuit was close at hand. The eagerly anticipated start of the Great Race was only moments away.

The field for tonight's competition is the largest of the season. Contestants have come to vie for the title from both the East and West coasts.

Unexpectedly, a nemesis of the champion by the name of Baby Lane suddenly appeared from out of nowhere. He was not expected to be in Las Vegas and surely not scheduled to race. As is usually the case at these gatherings, this resulted in an unauthorized side race before the main event.

Despite his better judgment, the champion initiated the challenge. In defense of his team colors, he sought retribution for the defeat of his protégé a few weeks earlier. Shakur decided to get off to a quick start against his opponent, since he had a reputation for delivering Crippling defeats and was known to be out for Blood.

Lane knew it was not in keeping with tradition to flash trophies won from rival competitors. Yet rumor has it that he was proudly showing everybody his stolen treasure - the legendary *Death Row Diamond*. This breach of etiquette did not go unnoticed by many of the other drivers. They also, decided to join in the race to reclaim the stolen prize.

The trophy was restored to its rightful owners. It was now time for the contestants to prepare for the night's real action.

Each driver has their own pre-race rituals. Although most of the West coast drivers get in the spirit by drinking a concoction known affectionately as *Thug Passion*. Occasionally they are known to pour spirits on the track to commemorate previously fallen drivers.

These races are usually dominated by sleek sports cars, but tonight for some reason Tupac chose a large luxury BMW 750i sedan as his steed. However his choice of vehicle did not alarm his fans in the least. He had been known to defeat other young challengers who raced in a more fast and furious style. It seemed that the champ's only trouble these days was his great rival - Mr. Big from the East.

Mr. Big was notorious for traveling in vehicles that were just as large and luxurious as the champion's. In Big's case however, it was obvious that he needed such a chariot to support his great countenance and accommodate his easy flow driving style. Their similarities made them formidable foes. Legend has it that they once had great respect for one another, but they were now fierce and bitter rivals.

The rules are unclear about this, but for this particular race, Tupac rode in the passenger seat rather than drive the car himself. He chose one Mr. Suge Knight, a major figure from the

West team to drive in his stead. This minor detail would ultimately have a considerable affect on the outcome of the race.

His choice of vehicle now made more sense, because Knight required a vehicle that provided him with a great deal of room to operate. He needed a ride in which he could work the controls utilizing his infamous underhanded driving technique.

Tupac's usual trusted second, one Mr. Yaki Kadafi, had been previously assigned to other duties.

Suge had proven in the past to be a master driver, although several of his own pit crew had left his team in the past. They claimed that while in the employ of Mr. Knight, they experienced a very hostile work environment. However as far as we know, Tupac had no such beef with Knight that night.

All were encouraged by the look on Suge's face. Most onlookers observed that he gave the impression that he had full command of the situation. There was no reason at the start to believe that Shakur's fate was not in good hands.

The racers for the main event took to the course in an unfamiliar fashion. They lined up one behind the other. Apparently the other participants had allowed Tupac to take the lead. They obviously hoped that his previous exertion of effort and the additional weight he was carrying would be his undoing. This tactic proved to be either a brilliant calculation by the other competitors, or an extreme error in judgment by Shakur.

Without warning, Suge brought the BMW to a complete stop, allowing four rivals to shoot by them on Tupac's side. One of the riders passed on Suge's side, but did not figure in the outcome of the race. This tactical faux pas would eventually cost Tupac the Great Race, although he did not concede defeat until almost a week later.

The aforementioned Mr. Big from the East was notably absent from the field, but it is believed that he had an unidentified challenger entered in the race. After the race was over, it remained unclear who this driver was. He also did not come forward to claim the victory. Mr. Big would not reveal whether he had a contestant entered, but it had been long rumored that he offered a large sum of money to anyone who would take the wheel in his absence.

This rumor had persisted since a race some years ago in which Tupac was passed by five drivers, but managed to recover and take the lead again. Some believe this to be mere speculation, since it would have been very difficult to plan such an operation. It had become more and more difficult in the weeks preceding the race for the Easterner's to make any arrangements to compete in the Western territories

It is still unclear whether Lane came to town specifically for the Great Race. However, there is little doubt that his earlier defeat might propel him to avenge that very bitter loss. He was not soon to forget his very public row with the members of "The Row".

It may be irrelevant that the winner of the race is still in question. The fact that the great Tupac was felled is not in question and was witnessed by all. The void he left in the sport after his departure has yet to be filled by anyone. To this day, none of his rivals have come forward to acknowledge their triumph.

Some of his fans were inconsolably affected by the outcome. They have taken to imagining he is still racing.

The race results will continue to remain in question. As is usually the case, there were no officials present when the race was decided. When they were asked to get involved in the disputed issue, they did not make much of an effort. They were rumored to have been paid in secret beforehand, to stay clear of the streets where the race took place. Others speculate that although the officials secretly enjoy these races, they have little regard for the participants that the sport attracts.

Much time has passed, the dust has settled and all the smoke has cleared. Still to this day we do not know who won the Great Race.

Shakur's once trusted second, Mr. Kadafi has offered his account of that night's events, but has since been forced to retire from the illegal street racing scene. He is no longer available for comment. A short time later both Mr. Lane and Mr. Big would also suffer similar defeats in the streets from which they would not recover.

The role Mr. Knight played in Tupac's crushing defeat would cause him to remain silent about his part in the Great Race forever. Some believe he is the only person who knows the identity of the actual winner.

Vince Vanguard Vainglorious
Vainglorious Press 2006

Brotherhood of the Rock

They say that - Those *that can't do, teach*....or some shit like that. Well there was a time when I could do – very well indeed, but there's only so much you can do with a basketball in the real world. I was definitely in the real world now. Thank God I graduated from college. At least that's what the piece of paper hanging on my Grandmama's living room wall says.

I stopped playing pro ball just before these new motherfuckers started making all of this ridiculous money. Just four years in the league and seven in Europe don't get you any kind of pension. I had run out of every basketball playing option there was now. NBA, Europe, CBA...., it was all over. I wasn't getting any younger either, so I did what I had to do.

Cesar Chavez Community College, the *Home of the Aztecs.* The home of my past glory. Now it was my future place of employment. *Seminar in Personal Development* was the only class I could teach without an advanced degree. If it wasn't for my boys staying on my ass to finish school, I probably wouldn't have any degree at all.

Basically, my job is to tell a bunch of kids who couldn't get into Cal, USC or UCLA that they can still be winners, even if they don't go to a four-year school. I'm also supposed to help them find a "career path" and try to make a difference in their lives. I guess I can do that.

If they knew what I know, they wouldn't be at this motherfucker in the first place. Junior College, shit I only came here to play ball. If I could have gone pro straight out of high school like they do nowadays I would have. Most of these fools are actually coming here to get an education. They're gonna get one allright, but not the one they were expecting.

They're gonna find out that for most of them, community college is just a two year break from the real world, filled with fuckin' dumb "Hood Rats". They'll probably even end up gettin' one of them pregnant. Oh yeah they'll get to smoke a bunch of "Chronic" and do a little light reading in between.

After the two years are up, they'll probably wind up with the same sorry ass job they would have got even if they didn't come here at all. Oh yeah, they're gonna have that dumb ass broad they got pregnant and a baby around for the rest of their life now and a big as high interest student loan to pay off. Now that's some adult education for yo' ass.

Now what they really want me to do is coach this year's new crop of part time *Crip Walkers, East L.A. Ese's* and the occasional 7 foot Rancho Cucamonga *Mandingo* who flunked the SAT. I am officially in charge of making sure the administration can stir up a new batch of the old "Aztec Pride". I guess I can do that. Having a winning basketball team is the best recruiting tool the school has going for it. It makes the kids feel like they go to a "real" school.

Don't get me wrong, I'm thankful for everything the school did for me. "C4" gave me a place to play until I got into Sonoma State. I would have played college basketball anywhere though. I love everything about basketball.

Basketball is the most beautiful sport known to man. Every nigga who can't play is jealous of every one who can. And boy were they jealous of me. I'm tall, slim, fine, good looking, strong and fast. I can jump over your ass, dribble around you, shoot over you, dunk in your face and there ain't shit you can do about it. Then after I win the game your woman wants to sleep with me.

It not just all that stuff though. I swear to God, there's something magical when you are out there on the court. Basketball players are special and everybody else knows it. They just might not admit they know it.

Football players need a coach or a quarterback to call the plays. Besides any fat bastard can do what they do. Baseball teams rely on a pitcher and the manager to run the show - the slowest show on earth. But basketball, man basket ball is 3 or 4 or 5 guys totally in sync, dedicated to one cause, playing with one ultimate purpose. Basketball is fast, it's powerful, it's beautiful – truly the greatest show on earth.

When it's really on and poppin', the entire team plays with one mind. Every man on the court can score. Every man on the court can win the game. Ever man can be a hero. At the same time, when the ball is in your hands, it's like you're the only man in the world. You can lose the ball. You can miss the shot. You can lose the game – all by yourself. But that's what you live for. That's what makes it so special.

Now if you play with a bunch of guys regularly like I do, then you always know what the other man can do and what he can't do. You never have to say a word to each other. You know what your man is thinking and feeling just by looking at him. It's like magic, real unity baby, like a strong family.

"Kuga", Joe, "Stic" and me were a family. We've have been playing ball together since high school. We all met in AAU ball. We were the very best.

Joe and Stic went to Crenshaw. Kuga and me went to Baldwin Hills. We beat Stic them for the state championship in '87. Them niggas are still salty about that. We still play together every Saturday at 3 o'clock up at Venice Beach like clockwork

Even when Kuga was on that crack rock, we knew he could still set a pick. When Stic was "locked down" for them 2 years, we played 3 on 3. No matter what, we always managed to keep the team together. That's what's called improvisin'.

After college, Joe made it to the CBA for a few years, but never broke into the "P's". He eventually learned how to do HVAC work. Now he's got himself a nice li'l family and a house in "the Wood". I've basically been pimpin' that local ex-NBA star shit and shackin' up with wannabe actresses and models since I got back from Europe. Now I got this gig at the school.

I always show up at the court a little early. I like to see what the competition is lookin' like. Now that I'm a "Big Time" college basketball coach, who knows, I might even spot some fresh talent out here. Three o'clock is our regular meeting time. That's usually when all of the gangsters are finished playing. It ain't as bad as it used to be up here, but it can still get a little rough. Some of these fools can play ball, but basically they just come to fight and will start some shit over the least little foul.

"Yo Ced!!!! Where is Kuga???? That nigga didn't ride wit' you????" Stic bellowed out from the sidewalk. Joe and Stic usually rode together, but you usually heard Stic's loud ass mouth before you saw him.

"I ain't heard from him today, but I guess he'll be here in a minute" I said.

"Well I'm ready to ball. My wife ain't been givin' me no pussy, so I'm gonna take some of this frustration out on these young niggas." Joe chimed in as he gyrated his badly aging hips.

"Nigga you ain't gone do shit. Anyway them gangstas still got the court so let's just wait for Kuga." I replied.

We sat on the bleachers and waited for Kuga. The sidelines and the grass were full of broads who liked to watch big thug ass niggas shoot ball with their shirts off. Not too many other cats were around. The ones that were didn't look much like ballers. We could probably get next up after this game was over and the gangstas would be leaving by then if they lost. That is if Kuga would bring his ass on. We were looking around for Kuga more than we were watching the game, so we didn't notice that the last game was over. The other team left and them gangstas were still holding court.

"Yo Dad!!!! Y'all got next????"

The first time a young cat called me "Sir", I didn't realize who the fuck he was talking to. I grew to accept Sir, but it was something about that "Player" and "Dad" and "Unc" shit that really fucked with me. In my mind I was still 19. In my mind I could still fuck this nigga's lady all night long, kick his ass and dunk in that motherfucker's face. In the real world, the blue rag stickin' out of the back pocket of his *Dickies* and the one wrapped around his teammates head made me decline to want to press either issue today.

"That nigga must be talkin' to you" Stic said to Joe.

"Naw man, I think that Nigga talkin' to Cedric, he da' one who teach li'l chillun now."

"We waitin' for our man to show up so we can play four on four Bro. We'll just wait" I responded.

"Yo fool, just pick one of these other busters up." He retorted. "Y'all gone lose anyway."

You see, this is why we usually don't play before Three o'clock. I guess these "Youngstas" had already hit a big lick last night, so they'd rather shoot ball than go shoot *Bloods* or gaffle a liquor store right now. It's not that we never play these fools, it's just that niggas got shit to lose now and it's no telling what might happen when you play wit' these niggas.

Stic had done a bid for theft by conversion when he was living with this "Breezy" that liked nice shit. She had him pussy whipped and willin' to do anything for her. Now he had his shit back together and was bartending and promoting for this L.A. dyke club down on Pico Boulevard. Kuga was doing substance abuse counseling at one of the rec' center programs I used to run back in the day. Joe was lost for a while after he didn't go pro, but Kuga showed him how to use one of them city programs to send him to HVAC school. Hell, I wouldn't have this new gig now if it wasn't for these Brothers.

I found out about the job at the school not because I was an alumnus, but because Stic was fucking this bisexual chick he met at the club. She happened to be an Assistant Coach of the men's team at the University of Los Angeles. She was offered the job herself, but she turned it down to wait for something bigger.

The bottom line is that we stick together and look out for each other, which is why we didn't like playing without Kuga. Besides, we always try to avoid playing any niggas with guns stuck down their ass cracks whenever possible. The thing was, now we were in a position where we could start some shit by playing or not playing. Especially if Stic said the wrong thing, which he had a bad habit of doin'.

We looked around to see if anybody looked like they were worth picking up. There was one dude sprawled across the bleachers on the other side wearing a hoodie pulled down over his head. He looked like he might be able to play. He was all slumped over, but he looked like he was about Kuga's size. Everybody else looked like point guards and shooters so we decided to go with this dude since we needed a big man.

"Where the fuck is Kuga…." Stic said under his breath before he yelled across the court"….Yo "Big Man"!!!!….You wanna run with us????" As he stood up, we all looked at each other like "*Damn*!!!!"

This kid was about nineteen, but if I was his Daddy I'd hate to be feeding and clothing his big ass 'cus he was about 6'10", 265 pounds and he wore about a size 19' shoe. "What's your name kid" Joe spoke to him like he was his Daddy. "Everybody just call me "Jungle" Ya feel me Folk????" Was what he said or what it sounded like.

Now even though I hated "Dad" "Pop" "Unc" or even "Sir" if it was said the wrong way. I kind of really feel disrespected when a young ass nigga calls me "Folk" or "G" or "Pimp", like I'm one of his homeboys. I'm a grown ass man and this generation's Mama's don't seem to be teaching their kids the difference.

We stuck our hands out to shake and in a few simple words explained our entire basketball history to him and his limited role in it. "Joe – Point" I said as I pointed at Joe. "Stic plays Power Forward, I shoot and you da "Big Man," Aiight????" I explained with no room for negotiation, as these roles had been reinforced by years of takin' cats to the hoop and bussin' many niggas asses. "Aiight" he said. That's all we needed to hear. Now it was on.

"We takin' it out. We da winners" Gangsta number one said with pride. "We go to 24 by two's out here "Dad" and ain't no threes so y'all old niggas gotta come in the paint." He said with a smile that meant it could get rough in there. He reminded me of Stic when he was young. He was slim and cocky with a big mouth and a game to match.

Most everybody who balls at the beach is good. You get ex-Pros like me, college players and ex-high school players, gangsters and cats with big game that never had the discipline to play organized ball. I wasn't sure which one Jungle was. I think he must've played some high school ball, but he seemed too "street" to be in college, but he didn't seem to know any of the gangstas, so I don't think he was *Blood* or "Cuzz".

Despite the warning about coming in the paint, so far it didn't matter. Big man was an absolute force down low and he set picks like a pro. Between his dunks and my shooting, we were up 10-6 and looking like our old selves with or without Kuga. Now Kuga was our man and with him we always knew what we were getting, but this man-child who called himself "Jungle" was no joke. He was big, quick and could shoot. He played like Dominique Wilkins in Karl Malone's body. "So y'all just gone let big man dunk and that's it????" The big mouth gangster laid down the challenge. "Let one of your boys do they' thang." He continued on.

Joe took the ball out up top and threw it in to Jungle. Jungle swung it to Stic then moved over and set a pick on Stic's man. Stic drove to the basket and went up and under the man on the left side of the basket and reverse slammed on him and the other guy down low. "Is that what you young niggas wanted to see????" Stic said in his usual brash way. Then he tapped the ball to the man who should have been checking him. This is why we play at Three o'clock and don't play these gangstas without Kuga. "Oh so ya'll da Lakers now ???? We got somethin' for that ass next time" *G number 1* said.

We took the ball out again. The score was 12-6 and this shouldn't take much longer. The last of the gangsters would be gone after these dudes lost. Joe took the ball out and threw a long pass to me as I drove to the basket. It was a little too long, but I managed to catch up to it in time to shovel it back to Jungle who was trailing me. He slammed it down with two hands, with all the authority of the king that was "Jungle". It was now 14 to 6.

Joe was still up top so he took the ball out again as usual. He threw it to Stic on the left wing and as Stic was about to jab step his way to the hole, Gangster #1 slapped at the ball and caught Stic dead in the eye. Stic lunged at him and tried to grab him around the waist, but Joe jumped in and pulled him away. As Joe pulled him away though, he left Stic in a position that let him get slapped in the face again.

All of a sudden this kid who we had never seen before, ran over to me and shouted "I got that nigga wit' all that mouth, you get the one wit' the rag on his head, ya boy can square up wit' that nigga who stole him and ya other man can deal wit' dat one!!!!"

Goddamn, General Kuga is that you????

The last thing I wanted to do was fight these youngsters, but it was pretty much no turning back now. Before we could even discuss the situation, Jungle rushed the nigga who had been talkin' shit all day and knocked his ass out cold as he yelled at him, "You thought y'all was just gone rush my nigga's and get away wit' it!!!!????"

Instead of coming to deal with me, my assigned man went to help his partner get up off the ground. As Stic and the cat that snuck him squared off Jungle came behind him and put him in a "Full Nelson." "Go on, buss that nigga back!!!!" Jungle yelled at Stic like he was a little kid. "Teach that nigga to respect his elders, Dad!!!!!" Stic slapped him a couple times and then told Jungle in a politely asking sort of way to let him go.

"You sure???? I got this nigga for you, Folk." Jungle assured Stic that he had his back. The loud mouth gangster and his boy had already bailed to the ride. The last two were outnumbered now and with Jungle's big ass on our side it was like more like 7 against 2, so they made their way to the whip post haste.

As Stic held his black eye he looked up at our new *best li'l big homey* and said "Goddamn "Big Man", you ain't shit to play wit' is ya????" Reaching forward to give Jungle a pound. "It ain't no thang, "Unc" I was jus' helpin' out my folks."

"Folks????" I rang in "Big man you don't even know us."

As he dusted off his new white Puma 94/50s he said "I know all of y'all, you my Uncle Andre's boys. Everybody 'round here know you. You Cedric Crawford, you signed my first ball when you was in the P's"

"Uncle Andre???? – Kuga????" Stic said.

"Yeah, dude. I remember you too. You used to get my Mama dem basketball shoes for me and all that other stuff when you used to sell that hot shit. I remember you too" He said to Joe, "You gave my Mama that information from the city about going to Medical Assistant school when my Pops broke out on us. I definitely know y'all all helped my Uncle get off that "Rock". We family "Cuzz." Family stick together. I came up here 'cus Andre said "Uncle Cedric" might be lookin' for some folks to play ball for the Aztecs. Is that real talk, Folk???? My Mama say I need to get my ass in school and do somethin' wit' my life"

"I guess so nephew, especially since we family and all" I said as everybody laughed while Stic was still holding his eye. "I just got one question for you though." Which was the question on everybody's mind on this lovely Southern California afternoon, so we all asked our new "Fifth Man" in unison?

"Where in the fuck is Kuga!!!!????"

Vince Vanguard Vainglorious

Vainglorious Press 2006

The Letter S

Salt, sugar, sex and smoke sustain society. They anesthetize the masses. Salt, sugar, sex and smoke help you stick to the routine. Toil to shop, shop 'til you drop. Salt, sugar, sex and smoke, they narcotize and pacify. Salt, sugar, sex and smoke fuel the sleep deprived sojourn of slavery.

"Same shit, different day" You say to yourself. In reality it's a siege of new shit, day after day, steering you closer and closer to your ultimate stress related stroke. You try to shake off the stress with each new day anyway you can. You seek to ignore the surreptitious, stealthy, staggering assault on your heart. Salt, sugar, sex and smoke, the true opiates of the people.

Take my man Stan for instance. Stan the man. Stan's a salesman. He wears the finest suits and very expensive shoes.

About ten o'clock each day, Stan takes his first snack break. He's still sleepy, so he staggers over to the snack machine to get his first salty, sugary snack of the day. Sometimes he even drinks a shot of single malt Scotch from the silver flask he keeps in his seersucker suit pocket to ease the stress of reaching his staggering sales quota.

He's not really hungry yet and lunch time will soon come, so he only scores a Snickers bar for this early morning sugar fix. Consumption time - approximately thirty seconds. One thousand calories and no nutrition. He's still not satisfied. Stan needs something else to stir his sin sick soul. Maybe a sexy sight will soothe his sinking state of mind.

"Shit, I still got 12 minutes left. I guess I'll go have a smoke." Stan says to himself. I forgot to mention, Stan's a cigarette smoker. He thinks sucking on those cancer sticks is going to soothe his stress. It does for a second, but it may add to a sickening death sentence later on.

He decides to stand outside the building near the solarium. Having secured a suitable spot to scope the honeys, he can smoke his satisfying Salem cigarette, with his buddy Steve from security. He stands in his usual spot so he can get a look at all of the sexy soul sisters from the service department.

"Damn that Sister over there is fine." Stan says to the other square smoking sucker Steve from security standing shoulder to shoulder next to him.

"Yeah, I think her name is Sheila," Steve says sharing in Stan's shameless sexual fantasy. "She is slammin'."

"No Shit." Stan says. "I sure would like to stick that."

"Fo' sheezy. Me too." Steve says to Stan even though they both know she'd never date a guy from security.

"Allright, I'll see you later Steve. I gotta go back upstairs and make some big stacks."

Stan says to Steve as if to signify his higher social standing and his ascending financial status.

"Sho' nuff. Same shit, different day" Steve says in sober acceptance of his lower social strata.

Stan's break is over now so he saunters back to his section to sustain his daily slave.

Finally lunch time comes. Stan walks quickly to the stairs, so he can stand in the shortest line at the sandwich and sundry shop downstairs. As he passes by the salads without giving them a second thought, he sees the slimmy Sheila from service that caught his eye before back at the solarium. He buys his sundries, his steak and cheese sandwich with fries and his Sprite and saunters over to a certain spot where chances are Sheila might sit down beside him. She sits with her back to him instead, so he has to devise some sly strategy to spit some slick game at her.

"Excuse me Miss; can you pass me a straw?" Stan says very studly.

"Sure, I can…." Sheila says very soft and sweetly.

"It's a pleasure to meet you. My name is Stan from corporate sales…."

(****See how smooth Stan managed to sneak in his high paying job in systems sales to help him snag sexy young Sheila????)

" ....What about Saturday night????.... "Sure is the Sambuca Club okay with you????"....

"Sure, that's a hot spot" Sexy young Sheila says sensing that she's snagged a smooth operator with a sense of style and the scrilla to match.

So there you have it. Stan the man's got some sexy new skins named Sheila scheduled for this Saturday night's sex session. And so it goes.

"Yeah girl, I'm goin'solo, no mo'....I'm gonna hold on to this nigga...Is he fine??? Girl please, and you know this...How long have we been talkin'????? Since last Monday, but shit I already know....His status???? I don't know how much money he makes. He works in systems sales, so I guess he makes pretty good money.....HIV status???? Girl what the fuck is you talkin' about, that nigga is clean from head to toe....Yeah I know you see all kinds of different people down at the clinic, but he ain't like that....Ok, I will girl....Allright, I said I'll ask him, Damn....I'll talk to you tomorrow girl.... Shiiit, I ain't gonna lie to you, I'll probably jus' call you Monday, 'cus tonight I know what it's gonna be and tomorrow I gotta get up and go to Sunday School....Okay girl, I'll talk to you later."

Sheila and Stan, young love in full bloom. Hot quick sex at lunchtime in the office building stairwell, wet and wild high times on the living room sofa and late nights spent making sweet love under satin sheets. Then all of a sudden, there are phone calls unreturned, no noontime rendezvous, no late night soul sessions and no early morning moanin'. Young love can be so fleeting. And so it goes.

….."Stan!!!! Stan!!!! Stan!!!!, I know you in there, answer the phone, it's Sheila!!!! I can see your Suburban sittin' outside. I bet you up there fuckin' some new skeezer. My girl Shirley says she saw you at the STD clinic. She says you got that shit!!!!....Stan!!!! Stan!!!! Stan!!!!"….

It seems what the old folks say is still true. What looks good to you ain't always good for you. Apparently, after a few weeks of slappin' skins, sittin' on faces, anal strokin' and Sheila suckin' on Stan's sick sex slinger unprotected, Sheila is now stuck with some shit she can't get rid of. Sweet young Sheila eventually confronts slick Stan, but he say's he didn't know he had that scary shit and it's not his fault that she didn't want to use the sheepskins when they were slippin' and slidin' away. Silly Sheila, did she really think slick shit talking Stan would come straight with her???? So now Sheila's left to face some really scary shit all by her lonesome, since Stan let it be known that his one and only plan is always just to stick and move.

As for Slick talking Suburban drivin' Stan the man who works in sales and makes stacks, Stan's still out there slappin' skins with any skeezer he sees. Still spreadin' that shit from stoop to stoop, slash to slash, snatch to snatch. Still shrivelin' his sick heart smoking them squares, suckin' down sugary soda, stuffin his stomach with salty snacks, slavin' for some mothersuckin' supremacist with no plans to save his own ass or his people.

Stan the man with the good job. Making the scene at all of the swankiest spots, every Saturday night. Settin' it off on the left and right, drinking shot after shot of single malt Scotch and Stoli' Vodkatinis, eating salty wing after wing, smoking' square after square, raw sexin' slimmy after slimmy, spreading his sick semen all over town, squirt after squirt and seed after seed. And so it goes.

The *Last Poets* once said that when the revolution came *we'd* be somewhere with "fried chicken hanging from our mouths". Well now we don't eat fried chicken in public, we eat shrimp scampi and sushi and drink Single Malt Scotch and Sake and the lunch counter isn't segregated anymore, but we're still fighting against all the same ole Shit!!!! This message is brought to you by salt, sugar, soulless sex, smokes, shots and stress. Consume all you can, you've earned it.

Vince Vanguard Vainglorious
Vainglorious Press 2007

Cigarette Money

I've been trying to get this broad's sharp ass elbow out of my ribcage since five o'clock this morning. The novelty of having a woman sleeping next to me for a change had worn off about two hours ago. I usually manage to make some excuse to get them out of here way before I have to deal with this kind of shit. I'll just slide out of bed and maybe she'll wake up from the movement and be ready to leave. If I pull the covers over her ass, she'll definitely notice when I turn the air off. *Damn, why do I continue to do this shit????*

As I exit the room I pick up the crumpled pack of *Mores* lying on the dresser. I walk towards the front door and remember my lighter is in my pants lying on the floor next to the bed. I walk back into the room and try to make enough noise to wake her up as I search for the lighter. No such luck. All I can do now is sit on the stoop and smoke for a minute until it's time to try again.

I stumble across the newspaper lying on the porch and decide to read to pass a little time. I need to wait just a little longer before I can politely put this broad out of my crib. It's about 6:45am, its light out, but not quite light enough. After all the good ass this girl put on me last night, I'd feel bad just kicking her out in the street all cold-blooded.

The front page of the paper says *BOMBING OF CAMBODIA ENDS.* Maybe Mr. Nixon's bullshit war will be over soon. Enough motherfuckers I knew had definitely already paid a high price for that shit. This broad who's in here fuckin' me, her ole man's probably over there right now dodging bullets while she was up in *J-Mo's* last night drinking up all of his allotment money. I wasn't really interested in that war shit since it didn't affect me, so I turned to the Business section to look at the *Wall Street*.

I wanted to see if my number had turned out yesterday. Before I could find it, the door opened and the girl from last night stepped out on the stoop. "I left my phone number on yo' dresser. I hope you don't mind, but I took a couple dollars for cigarette money off the nightstand too." Before I could fix my mind to say anything, she bent down and kissed me real sweet on my cheek and walked down the stairs. "See ya" She said with a wink. As drunk as I was last night, I didn't ever get a good look at this broad's face. As she walked down the street, I figured I could spot her by that fine ass if I ever saw her again.

The coast was clear now, so I decided I'd go back inside and try to get a little bit of sleep…. alone. I lifted the ashtray up to see how much money she took and like she said it was only a few dollars so I said fuck it and fell asleep. I wake up a little bit later feeling pretty rested. I don't recover from a night of fuckin' the way I did when I was younger. My good mood changes when I look at the clock and see that it's damn near three o' clock. "Goddamn!" I remembered that I was supposed to meet Vicki down at Hahnes to buy the kids some school clothes today at two o'clock.

As sweet as she was when I first met her, she don't forgive me shit now that we ain't together anymore. I try to call her, but there's no answer. She's either still at the store or on her way back home. Either way she'll be mad as hell no doubt. The kids are probably a little pissed too.

Kenya is just like her Mom and when her Mama gets mad at me she tries to imitate her, which coming from a seven year old girl is kind of cute. Malik is my li'l partner. He'll be mad too, but all I have to do is take him to play some ball and we'll be *runnin' in the cut* buddies again in no time. Vicki though, "Goddamn!!!!" I hate to hear her mouth when she gets goin'.

"Was probably fuckin' some ugly 'ho all night long…. I bet you ain't never late to hang wit' them tired ass niggas at *J-Mo's*….How much money you got left anyway????..." I know I'm gonna hear all that shit plus some more.

I wanted to take the bus over to Washington Avenue where Vicki lives but damn if that girl didn't take all my loose change too. I didn't feel like stopping to make change and didn't want to bust a $20, so I decided to foot it all the way to the "Woods" over in the Fourth Ward where Vicki lives.

The "Woods" is what everybody calls the Carter G. Woodson Projects. They ain't the worst in the world, but I really don't like the idea of my babies living there when they could be living with me in the house my Mama and Daddy left me. Vicki won't hear none of that though. She's a good mother and I see my kids whenever I want to, but not letting 'em live with me is her one way of fuckin' with me.

I finally get there and damn if they ain't here. I know I'm in the wrong about this shit, but I'm kind of pissed that I walked my ass all the way over here. It's hot as a sonofabitch out here and I had to climb up three flights of rickety stairs and they ain't even here. *Goddamn!!!!*

As I'm leaving the complex, I see Kenya and Malik playing on the swings. They must have just got back from the store. "Hey babies - where's ya Mama????" I ask as I kiss them on the foreheads. They're trying to "mean mug" me so they don't say anything. They just point over to the building where the mailroom is. I go over there and surprisingly, she ain't quite as pissed as I thought she would be, but she is a little salty.

"Nigga where have you been???? Anyway, if we leave now we can get back down there before they close. All the good stuff's probably already gone though. I hope you late 'cus you stopped by *Curt's* to get my money." She said without looking up as she fingered through the stack of bills and junk mail.

What the fuck is she talking about???? "Have mercy - I knew that "bad boy" was gone fall….Malik, Kenya, let's go!!!!" She calls to the children as she continues to rattle on"…..814 my lucky day, my lucky number." All of a sudden I realized what she was talkin' about. In my post pussy funk, no sleep gettin', elbow cutting in my back, early morning stupor, I didn't realize that the slip for the number Vicki told me to play was also gone from under the ashtray too. Just a few dollars for cigarette money my ass. *Goddamn!!!!*

"I forgot to stop by Curt's 'cus I was trying to get down to the sto' and meet ya'll" I say as I search her face to see if she can tell that I'm lying. Apparently she buys it so I go on to say, "Baby take this $20 and y'all go to *McDonald's* and I'll meet you at Hahnes after I stop by *Curt's* and get yo' money." She looks at me half disgusted and half anticipating the eventual arrival of her ghetto lottery money. "Allright man, but you know they close at six????" I wave bye to my babies and head back to the house to make sure I didn't leave the slip in my other pants or something.

On the way home I stop by *Curt's* just to let him know I'd be back for my money. I walk through the door and go down the "Soul Train" line and greet various "Bloods" "Blacks" and Bros". I arrive at Curt's chair and give him his much deserved "My Main Man Soul Brother Shake."

Curt's barbershop was the fulcrum on which the wheels of the neighborhood's underground economy turned. You could play the numbers here, cop a bag of *Bo Red Ses weed*, and even buy a hot ride wit' clean tags. The numbers was the bread and butter of this little enterprise though.

Curt ran numbers for BJ or "Big Jumpy" to you if you really knew the nigga. BJ was the kind of nigga you really wasn't sure whether you was supposed to speak to him or you wasn't. Either choice might be wrong and could get you fucked up. They called him *Big Jumpy* because that big "MF" would jump on anybody whether he knew they was carrying a piece or not.

"What's up Blood, how you be????" Curt says in his usual barber cum player style. He didn't go for bad and was a pretty cool cat on the whole, but with BJ's protection, he could damn near say or do anything he wanted to (which he did) around here. "I guess you came here to get yo' money....Mr. Big Time."

I can't believe this shit. I ain't hit the number in God knows when, I really need the money and Vicki's gone kick my ass. "Yeah Curt man that's what I need to talk to you about. I ain't got the slips on me and I don't know if I can get back down here before you close." It's just my luck that he is in a really generous mood. "Ain't no thang man. I can give it to you tonight if you gone be at *J'Mo's*. I wouldn't ordinarily do it for you, but BJ's baby Brother just got back from *the Nam* so we in a celebratory mood - you dig????"

I'll be damned; if I can find the ticket I might actually be able to fix this shit. "Solid Black???? That would be right on time. I'll see you like what, 11 – 11:30???" I ask. "Be cool nigga, I got you" he says as I start out the door.

As I walk out the door I run into this cat named Billy I grew up with. I couldn't get caught up talking to him. If I did I'd be stuck there listening to him carry on all day.

"What's Up Billy???? Man I gotta holla atchu later." I say as I slide him some dap and try to walk past quickly. "Damn nigga, you movin' mighty fast. I'm surprised you can walk at all after fuckin' wit' that broad Thelma last night." I make an about face. "Thelma???? You know that broad, Billy." Apparently he'd seen me walking out of *J'Mo's* with her last night. He laughs with his hand over his mouth as his imagination admires my dirty work from last night.

"Damn nigga, I didn't know you was Mackin' like that. You didn't even ask her name???" I remembered now that she did say her name was Thelma.

"Naw man it ain't like that. I was just drunk you know, so I forgot" "Hey, uh you know where she stays???" I didn't care what else he was thinking; I just had to find this girl so I could get Vicki's money. "I think she stays over there in Woodson Court, but best bet she'll probably be at *J-Mo's* tonight. You know BJ's gone be in there dropping a lot of bread 'cus his li'l Brother's comin' home from Nam." He was probably right I thought, but I couldn't really wait that long. "Bet man, you probably right. I'll be there tonight fo' sho'"

I finally make it home and damn if I don't look for them slips everywhere. Now Vicki always played 814 on August 14th. That was her Daddy's birthday. She played her Momma's `birthday too, but for some reason she always felt like her Daddy's was the lucky one. I don't see why because it never fell before until this time.

The kids start school in a few days and I haven't bought them any school clothes yet. I had some money to put on the number, so I played it too. No money for the babies' school clothes, my money's gone too and I got to explain this shit to Vicki. Goddamn!!! "She's going to kill me". I say out loud hoping for divine intervention from nobody in particular.

I decided to lie down for a while because all I had left to do today was go back to *J-Mo's* tonight. I had to be prepared to stay there all night if I had too. I couldn't go see Vicki again until I had that money. I lay down for a while, but not as long as I had planned to. I'm laying there thinking about all the different scenarios as I smoke me a "square". Then I remember that broad Thelma said she left her number on the dresser. Shit, I realize I can just call her.

I find the piece of paper then dial the number praying she picks up so I can put an end to this shit. The phone rings and a voice answers, but it ain't the sweet voice of the girl I was bonin' all last night. "Who is this!?!?!?!?" Damn, this nigga had the kind of voice that you could tell he was a big motherfucker, probably a stone cold killer and holding long conversations wasn't his strong suit. I hang up without saying anything, not believing the trouble my dick had got me into last night. I wasn't in the mood to go back to sleep so I decided I'd tip back over to Vicki's and just tell her the truth about what happened.

Walking back to Vicki's I wasn't upset with Thelma for what she did as much as I was pissed at myself. I thought about all the shit that caused Vicki and me to break up. Now I'm stuck fuckin with these over the hill *bar cocks* and *hole in the wall floozies* every Friday and Saturday night.

That wasn't what really bothered me though. What really bothered me was the way my babies was giving me them mean looks. Even though they was just looking mean like their Mama told them to, I could still remember how my babies was looking at me sitting on them swings. Don't get me wrong, I'm a pretty good Dad. I never miss one of Kenya's talent contests and I come to all of Malik's games and stuff. School is where I really want them to do big things though and I should never let nothing fuck me up from helping their Mama buy them school clothes and shit. I don't want either one of my babies to ever feel like they can't hold their heads up high.

I finally make it back to the "Woods" and I see BJ and Curt haulin' ass out of the parking lot in BJ's gangsta ass *Deuce and a Quarter* coupe. I walk up the lane towards Vicki's crib and I see her standing outside smoking a *Viceroy* talking to somebody sitting on the steps. She turns her head and sees me coming. "Girl I'll talk to you later." She's headed my way and I can see she ain't happy. "All right girl. I'm gone go up here and see if this fool done cooled off yet. Back home one day and already trippin'." Her friend says as she climbs the stairs. "Allright girl, go handle yours." Vicki says as she's about to handle me.

"Man what is this about you can't find my play slip????"

What the fuck???? In all my years I'd never known her to be psychic. "BJ and Curt jus' came by here to see BJ's brother and Curt said you was in the shop talkin' bout you won, but you didn't have the slips on you." *Goddamn!!!!*

"Baby its cool. I'm gone meet them at *J-Mo's* tonight and get the money." That only answers one part of the question and Vicki ain't never been no fool.

"OK so where the slips at, 'cus I can just take mine. Can't go to the store before Monday now anyway." She's right about that.

"Girl, why would I be walkin' around with 'em???? Curt said I can't get the money until tonight." Allright, score one point for me.

"Then what you doing over here now for." I ain't got much left and this shits got to end.

"Baby, I felt real bad about not getting the kids their clothes so I came over here to explain to 'em. You know I can't stand my babies being mad at me" Got out of that one. Muhammad Ali would be proud of me.

"They ain't here I let 'em spend the night with 'Fonso them." Alfonso was her gangsta ass cousin who had two kids about the same age.

"Girl I told you I don't like them goin' over there. I don't know what that niggers into, but I know it ain't good. I'll holler at you later then." I was pissed about my kids being in that environment, but I really just wanted to turn the tables so I could make a hasty retreat.

It's Saturday night and most niggas are out making their last hurrahs before they have to get ready for work on Monday – the ones with jobs. I walk in and all the usuals are here and quite a few more. Everybody heard BJ was gonna be throwing around some heavy bread tonight.

Soon as I walk into the club I run into that loudmouth fool Billy. This time I'm glad to see him for a change.

"Hey, there he is. My man James. How you be???" I signal the bartender to give me two Pabst's. "Billy my man, uh you seen that girl Thelma????" I grab the two *PBR*s from Otis and hand one to Billy. I know now he'd tell me anything I needed to know. "Shit man, everybody's seen her fine ass. She sittin' over there with Curt, BJ and her ole man. You know her man, that nigga BJ's baby brother Sam. As soon as I saw that nigga sittin' across the club, I remembered who he was - "Body Slam" Sam. He and BJ had kicked every niggas ass this side of Newark. Before I could even figure out how I was going to play this, Curt called me over to the table. "Mr. Big Time!!!! Bring yo' ass over here nigga!!!!"

I sit down with my Pabst. Everybody else is drinking Cold Duck and Crown Royal. "Get you some of this Duck nigga!!!! Curt say you 'bout to get paid," BJ says. *Goddamn!!!!* "Yeah Sam this is the nigga I was telling you about came in Curt's shop trying to get paid $6,000 wit'out no slip. You know you met his old lady Vicki earlier. She stay 'cross the way from Thelma." Big mouth nigga jus' addin' fuel to the fire.

That's right you heard him, I put $9 on it for me and played $1 on it for Vicki. It was her number and it came straight. I usually only play a dollar too, but for some reason this time I decided to put $9 on it. BJ and Curt pay $600 on a dollar straight bet, or $6,000 to a nigga whose ten slips ain't in the purse of a killer's ole lady.

As I was trying to figure out what to do next, all of a sudden some nigga at the table who I didn't even know chimed in. "Yeah, must have been this nigga's lucky day yes'erday 'cus I seen him walk outta here last night with this fine ass broad." If his eyes could talk, everybody would have heard them say - *Yeah I know what you did nigga and now I'm gone tell er'body.* Before this nigga could say anymore than he should, then Thelma turned the air conditioning off and pulled the covers over me.

"Mr. Lucky, huh???? I thought y'all said my girl Vicki was his old lady????"

"Uh, we separated." I said.

"So I guess you just thank you got a free pass to fuck ever thang walkin' now, don't you???? Probably tell 'em all kinds of shit to get 'em back to yo'crib, then kick 'em out of bed before the sun come up. I bet if they ain't ready to wake up, you might even turn off the A/C so they ass burn up and shit" Damn this bitch is crazy.

Then that big nigga Sam jumped in. "Ah girl, leave that nigga alone. Anyway why you care what that man do??? He just being a man. What you ought to be worried about is making sure whoever that nigga was that called today don't call my house no mo'."

I just knew what ever would be said next was gonna get me killed. Before anybody else could say another word though, Curt saved the day. "Allright, allright that's enough of this shit!!!! Y'all stay out of my man's business. Ain't nobody got time for this shit anyway, we got serious drankin' to do." It was obvious he'd done some serious drankin' already. God bless him.

Thelma still had more to say, but it wasn't what I expected. "Yeah and I'm ready to dance." She said as she tried to pull Sam's big, drunk, fresh back from Viet Nam crazy ass out of the booth. "Dance, shiiii-iiiit, I'm drunk. Dance wit' that nigga" He said as he pointed his inch thick trigger finger straight at me.

Thelma enthusiastically and I reluctantly made our way to the dance floor. It was just my luck that damn if they don't change up to slow songs as soon as we get the fuck up out of the booth. Now here goes Billy Paul's smooth ass adding to my worries, singing about *Me and Mrs. Jones got a thing going on...* I had no idea what that fool I didn't know was gonna say back at the table while we were gone either.

I try to hold her lightly but she presses her body up against mine tightly. She was holding me just like she did all last night. This broad is going to get my Black ass killed.

"Damn baby, you tryin' to give 'em a show ain't you."

"So Vicki's your old lady, huh????" It was clear she was not interested in anything I had to say.

"Yeah, my ex old lady"

"So why you out here fucking around on her???"

"Look I said she's my ex. You on the other hand, you got a husband, that big money nigga BJ is yo' Brother-in-Law so you ain't broke and you out here fuckin' around on ya man and takin' nigga's money. Besides, fuckin' around on yo' old lady don't give you no right to steal my play slips. Now do it????"

"Listen here Honey, yesterday my man was on the other side of the world but yo' old lady was right over there in the "Woods" takin' care of them sweet babies, trying to make something out of 'em while you was out here ho-hoppin'. Now look nigga, since Vicki's my girl, I'm gone give you back these slips, but let me ask you two questions. "

I'm not sure I want to know what the questions are, but I agree to answer.

"Which one of these slips is yours???? Is it the nine dollar one or is it this one dollar slip???? You do know she wants to put a down payment on a house for them children????" She asks me.

I release my arms from around her waist, "Nine dollars was hers, and the dollar was mine. Now what's the other question????"

She starts to slip the tickets into my pocket, "What are you gonna do with your $600????" She says as she pushes the two slips all the way down into my pocket.

I was a little pissed, but the only thing I could say through my tight jaw and clenched teeth was "I'm gonna buy my babies some school clothes, some shoes and some other stuff. If that's okay with you????"

The song ends as does our negotiation. Thelma and I walk back to the booth having settled our business. Everybody seems cool at the table too. Now I can get my money and call it a night. Everything was back to normal in Newark. As I reach in my pocket, I notice she even gave me back the three dollars for the cigarette money.

Vince Vanguard Vainglorious
Vainglorious Press 2006

Pretty Girls

My bus passes by Tabitha's house every morning, but it does not stop there.

Her father drives her to school so the Tall Boys can't get to her.

She'll be waiting for me as usual, by the big stone lion at the top off the stairs.

I hope she brought some cigarettes and some cookies to eat in homeroom.

I know she talks to those Black Barbie Dolls before I get here everyday.

Talking about cute boys and their fast bikes and shiny cars.

Those are the girls that always ask her why she hangs out with a "Girl like her."

Sometimes I think that "**T**" may really be one of them.

Longing for Pompoms and Proms and Tall Boys.

Sometimes I wish that I longed for those things too.

They just don't matter to me the way they do to her.

I guess I have to give David an answer about the Prom soon.

My Mom says I have to go.

That ignorant boy with the big head and the little ears will probably still be standing over her when the bus pulls up.

Talking about absolutely nothing, leaning against the light post saying all kinds of stupid shit.

I try to guess what she's going to wear to school every day and I try to wear something to match.

Sometimes I get it right, except when she wears one of those Tall Boy's jackets and her tight black jeans.

I know she doesn't wear his jacket to spite me.

Sometimes I'm not sure if she thinks about it at all.

The bus pulls up in front of the school, but she's not sitting on the wall.

The Pretty Girls are all sitting on the benches pointing at magazine photos of dresses and shoes.

I walk inside the school and peek inside the Girl's bathroom.

Maybe she slipped inside to take off those black church stockings her Mom sometimes makes her wear.

She's not in there.

I'm starting to have a nicotine fit now and a feeling I can't name yet.

One day I will be able to name this feeling all too well.

I walk back outside and sit next to the lion on the other side of the steps.

Maybe I'll hide behind the lion and play a trick on her.

I can see the parking lot much better from this side of the steps.

Now I'll have plenty of time to hide when her Dad's car pulls up.

I hear that Tall Boy with the big head and the little ears motorcycle coming down the street.

At least I got here first today.

Now I can save her from having to listen to all of his stupid bullshit.

She always manages to make herself laugh at his ignorant jokes.

Referring metaphorically to his dick like he's a fucking comedian.

He screeches into the lot and revs up his engine one last time.

That's how he announces his arrival to the other Tall Boys and Pretty Girls.

Then I see "T" get out of one of the Black Barbie Doll's car.

She walks up to the Tall Boy with the motorcycle and stands on her tiptoes to kiss him.

I walk inside to take my seat for homeroom.

I stare at the door for what seems like an eternity.

I hope desperately that my eyes were playing tricks on me.

I close them tight.

I imagined she would walk through the door wearing a different outfit.

Not wearing her white mini skirt and pink and black Pumas with the pink laces.

The same outfit I saw that girl wearing who kissed the Tall Boy on the bike.

As the door swings open David walks through and sits behind me.

He seems upset that I haven't given him an answer about the Prom yet.

"T" walks in and sits on the other side of the room so I can talk to David first.

As he taps me on the shoulder, I look at her thinking that we need to talk now.

She gestures to me that she will tell me about everything later.

I told David yes I'd go to the prom, but I don't remember turning around.

I don't remember taking my eyes off of her brown crossed legs and those pink laces.

Vince Vanguard Vainglorious

Vainglorious Press 2007

Scratchin' and Survivin' (Part I) Shot Caller

"A Man". "The Man". "Da Man".

He heard that word "Man" almost from the very day he was born. He heard it as soon as he could cry and before he could talk. Certainly before he could pee straight. Definitely before he knew what it meant to be "A Man".

"Little Man". "Mama's Little Man". "Daddy's Little Man".

"Ah go 'head on woman, one sip a beer ain't gone hurt the li'l nigga. It'll make "A Man" out of him."

"You got yo'self some girlfriends yet "Li'l Man"???? You gone be a "Ladies Man" ain'tchu????"

"Boy wipe yo' damn face and act like you "A Man"!!!! Mama ain't raisin' you to be another "Weak Ass Man"!!!!"

"Smart Young Man", that time when he got an A in school. Got yo'self a "Fine Young Man" they'd say when Mama's old girlfriends would give him those odd looks. They looked him up from his big feet to his bright eyes and handsome face and back down from his zipper to his big feet again. He was a "Young Gentleman" if he kept his Sunday clothes clean all the way through church or helped his Grandmama with her groceries.

"Big Man". "Boss Man". "Brother Man".

Uncle Curtis kept asking him if he'd gotten "some" yet, long before he knew what "it"
even looked like. When Mama's boyfriends met him for the first time, they would always
comment with a mix of surprise and disappointment that he was big enough to be
working with the men down at the stockyards. He noticed they seemed a little scared of
him too, even though they were grown men and he was only about thirteen. Mama used
to repeat their words about going to work sometimes when she lost her patience with him,
which always seemed to be after she lost her job or between paydays.

That first girl called him "Lover Man". He was only about fifteen, so he really liked that.
It seemed like she wanted a Daddy more that a lover though. Her mother even treated
him like he was her "Special Man" too. It seemed like she couldn't wait 'til they were all
one big happy family. She really just wanted "A Man" in the house that she didn't have
to be bothered with, but who could pay all the bills.

The girl used to tell him that her Daddy had left them because he wasn't much of "A
Man". When the girl got pregnant, she realized that Tut wasn't ready to be much of "A
Man" yet either. The baby came too early. Thank God she *lost* it.

He was just another "Sorry Man" when he dropped out of school. A big ole "Trifilin'
Man" when he couldn't find a job. A "Bad Man" when he beat that nigga half to death in

a dice game. Considered an "Unidentified Armed and Dangerous Man" when he shot his way out of that undercover bust. Just another "No Good Man" when he finally went to jail.

That Muslim in the joint tried to make him believe he was some new shit called a "Proud Black Man." The guards and the parole board made him realize he was just "Black". The chaplain tried to turn him into a "Good Christian Man". All of the rapes and shanks and killings he saw eventually made him lose his religion.

Even for somebody his size, it was a daily struggle to keep from becoming somebody's bitch, which is as far as you can get from being "A Man" in prison. To hold on to his "manhood" he had to beat the shit out of the top dog in there, a nigga named Rip. That was the first time he felt what it was like to be "Da Man". He would never forget that feeling.

When he came home from jail, at first he didn't feel like much of "A Man" at all. Even though he was about twenty-one now and even the government said he was one. He couldn't even get a job down at the stockyards. Before he went to jail he figured that he and the stockyards always had a date with destiny. Now that he was an ex-jailbird, even slicing up pig parts was off the table.

He couldn't find a job to save his life. Not being able to make any money was all he could think about. "A Man". "The Man". "Da Man". Certainly before he could pee straight. Definitely before he knew what it meant to be "A Man". He figured out pretty early on that being "A Man" was all about making money.

Before his Daddy left it was all he and his Mama ever talked about. She would constantly remind him, "That boy in there is eating like a racehorse and shittin' up diapers like one too!!!!" We need some mo' money comin' in 'round here!!!!" "What kind of "A Man" are you????" Daddy would insist that he was "All Man", but he couldn't make any more money than he did because of "The Man".

His Daddy's friends would always remind him that "Yeah man, that li'l nigga Tut is almost big as you." "Shit, he probably gone be whuppin' yo' ass pretty soon." Daddy vehemently denied that his "Li'l Man" would ever be able to whip his ass. In the back of his mind he must have felt differently. In any event he eventually decided that feeding another person who was big enough to whip his ass just didn't make much sense anymore. Either that or I guess he felt like there was only room for one Man in the house. So one day he up and split.

When Mama would bring home one of her new boyfriends, the cats would always look at him like he was doing something bad by eating up food they were planning on eating and sleeping in the room they had planned on playing spades and shooting craps in with the fellas. Then there were the times when there was no "New Man" around or one had just quit her. His mama would yell just like she used to yell at Daddy when he was around.

Sometimes she'd just cry. When she yelled, it wouldn't be at anybody in particular. She'd just be yellin'.

"Eating up all my food like a Goddamned horse and goin' through shoes like one too!!!!" "Lord I tell you, I don't know how we gone make it 'round here!!!!" That's when he realized what it really meant to be "A Man".

She never told him he needed to be the one to go out and get the money, but it was clear that there would be a lot more of it around if he could stop eating and growing so fast and chasing away her "New Old Man". He couldn't care less about chasing away her men, but he felt bad about having to eat and grow all the time and watch his Mama cry about it. He didn't do it because he didn't love his Mama. He just couldn't help it.

He was about thirteen when he first started bringing a little money home. She figured that at the worst he was just stealing like all the other li'l boys. When he stopped going to school that next year, she figured he was eventually going to stop going to school anyway like all the other li'l boys. Tut was never quite like all of the other li'l boys though.

She would hear all these scary stories from her girlfriends about all the things Tut was doing out in the streets. She figured that at least he wasn't shootin' up dope like all those other li'l boys. When he finally went to jail the first time, his Mama washed her hands of him. She turned her back on him, just like the mothers did all the other li'l boys.

He had already figured out that being "A Man" was about being alone though, so it didn't hurt him as much as it did some of the other li'l boys.

He never understood exactly why, but the other little boys were always a little scared of him. Even the teachers and the "big boys" treated him a little differently than the other little boys. The "big boys" would let him tag along when they went to fight against one of the other neighborhoods. His buddies always made sure he was with them when they went to go see some girls in the wrong 'hood. Sometimes he would make mistakes betting when he played spades, or forgot his point when he threw dice. Rarely did anybody ever point out his blunders.

One day when he was about seventeen, he went with his buddy to see these particular "ladies" who had their own place. His buddy said that they might have to give 'em a "li'l somethin'" since they were grown and not like the girls they were used to. He realized pretty quickly that they liked him more than they did his buddy. His buddy had a good rap, but the girls liked the way Tut walked the walk. There was something about his size and strength and good looks that made them feel very comfortable. Eventually he figured out that all he had to do now was learn how to talk to them like his buddy. After he learned how to talk the talk, there wasn't any woman he couldn't have or anything he couldn't make them do for him.

One day when he was about eighteen, this dude he hardly knew paid him just to ride with him to pick up some money. The dude handed the guy a package, but the guy didn't hand the dude the money right away. The dude pointed at Tut in the car and said something to him. Then the guy handed him the money. After that Tut would ride with the dude all the time.

One day, Tut rode with the dude to go see "The Man" who would give the dude the package to go take to the guy. Then one day Tut came inside with the dude and met "The Man" for himself. "The Man" thought Tut was smart and really took a liking to him. For once in his life "The Man" treated him like "A Man". Tut knew it was because "The Man" thought he could make a lot of money for him.

Eventually, one day Tut got the bright idea to go see "The Man" by himself. He wanted to see if he could get his own package. He realized that the only reason the guy would pay the dude for the package he got from "The Man" was because the guy saw Tut sitting in the car and thought that Tut was "Da Man". So Tut decided he could really be "Da Man" if he had his own package which he had to get from "The Man".

The dude was highly upset when he found out that Tut was trying to be "Da Man" by getting his own package from "The Man" to take to the guy. The dude tried to start some shit with Tut to keep him from becoming "Da Man". Eventually "The Man" called for a meeting between Tut and the dude, because both of them fighting to see who would be "Da Man" was hurting "The Man's" business. After the meeting between Tut, the dude and "The Man" nobody ever saw the dude again. So now Tut was officially "Da Man".

The thing about being "Da Man" though is that eventually you're gonna want to be "The Man", which is the hardest thing in the world to become. Even after all the ho's he'd pimped, dope he'd sold, numbers he'd ran, money he'd stole and niggas he'd killed, Tut still wasn't quite "The Man". Ever since he could cry, before he could talk, and certainly since his Daddy left home all Tut ever wanted to be was "A Man".

He felt like "A Man", but he still had to buy his dope from "The Man". He still had to pay "The Man" to let his ho's walk the street on their beats. When he collected the protection money from the stores in the neighborhood, he still had to pay his share to "The Man" who lived in the suburbs. Worst of all, "The Man" would always have the power to lock his ass up and throw away the key if he ever found himself back in "The Man's courtroom.

He'd finally found a way to become "The Man" this time though. "The Best of the Best Kansas City Nine Ball Tournament". This was it. This was everything he had ever dreamed of. This is what he went to jail for. What he'd killed for. What he'd gotten shot for. What he'd kicked all these ho's asses for.

In one night he was going to become a millionaire. He was gonna be a "Rich Man". He could finally show his Mama that he was a "Real Man". Everybody in the world would know he was a "Big Man". He could finally be "The Man." He wasn't going to let anybody or anything keep him from that.

Scratchin' and Survivin' (Part II) Behind the Eight Ball

Tut was bankrollin' him, so he'd already lost even if he wins. He damn sure was gonna lose if he lost. If he won he'd feel like a winner, but then he'd still have Tut leanin' on him for the rest of his money. Scratch already owed him money from various favors, loans and bad bets in the past. The old debts plus what it cost to stake this game was just enough to keep him a slave forever.

Scratch knew better than to fuck with Tut's money too. He'd gotten his ass whupped or his hands broken on more than one occasion in the past. I remember once when I was a kid, he got beat up so bad he was laid up in St. Luke's for almost two weeks. Mama said it wasn't St. Luke's, but he went to St. Louis to see about a job. Shiiiit, a job, she coulda done better than that. Scratch was a pool hustler.

In Kansas City, a pool hustler gets more respect than a preacher or a pimp. A good one could make more money than both. They definitely talk more shit. When Scratch was on his game, he could hustle more money than any preacher and he had more ho's than any pimp. For most niggas in KC, making money was their biggest problem. For Scratch having too much money was his.

It was a vicious cycle. When he was winning he had big money and he liked to throw it around. If he took a nigga's money on the pool table one minute, the next minute he'd be buying that same nigga a drink or sharing his needle with him. Every night was a competition between the bartender, the heroin dealers and the ho's to see who'd take his last dime. The broads and the booze jockeys, he'd heard all their shit before. It was usually the "Horse" traders whose lines he fell for the hardest.

What started out as a chicken shit habit when he was a young man, turned into a full blown King Kong Gorilla Jones when he got older. When he was high, his stick skills was suspect. Being a junkie and a pool hustler didn't leave him with a lot of career options either.

My Mama was always good to us when Daddy was sittin' in high cotton, but when the money got short so did her patience. Mama wasn't a junkie, but she was one of those broads that was just runnin' after Scratch for his money. After she got pregnant she figured being Scratch's old lady was an easier hustle than sittin' up on them bar stools waiting to see what kind of niggas was comin' up in "Smiley's" every night. Prince Charming was in short supply in Kansas City, Missouri, so Joe Willie Evans would have to do for now.

After the money ran out, she ran out too. One night when they were both out chasing them ghosts, I went over to my Aunt Retha's house. I convinced myself that I thought I heard somebody tryin' to break in. It was probably just one of Daddy's friends shootin' up in back of the house. I really just wanted a reason to leave. It just so happened that night Mama wasn't planning on ever coming back home. The next morning, Daddy decided it was best to leave me where I was. From that day on, I lived with my Aunt

Retha. That was the happiest day of my life.

When I was growing up, Aunt Retha tried to keep me out of the pool halls. I guess hustlin' was in my blood though. Daddy would come over to Retha's every once in a while and give her money when he remembered. Sometimes we'd go places together. The only places he really knew were the "shooting galleries", Smiley's and the pool room down by 18th and Vine though. He wanted to be a good Daddy, so because it was usually the middle of the day, he usually took me to the poolroom instead of the bar. He never took me to the shooting gallery. The pool room is where he taught me how to hustle.

"Chalk up too much and a nigga'll think you ain't sure about your shot."
"Remember Jo-Jo, jus' 'cus a motherfucker's drunk, don't mean he can't still shoot."
"Don't be one of them nigga's scared to scratch on the eight ball."
"Scared money can't make no money."

That was my Daddy's advice growing up. It wasn't no Ward Cleaver shit, but it helped me through some serious situations over the years. If you understand the code of the pool hall and how to work that table, there really ain't shit else in this world you need to know. Daddy taught me that sometimes you gotta shoot hard, sometimes you gotta shoot soft and sometimes you gotta put some "English" on yo' shit. Most importantly he taught me that if you always scared of missing the shot, you ain't got no chance to win.

Taking chances was how he got the name "Scratch". Joe Willie would take the most dangerous shots any nigga ever attempted. He never worried about scratchin', balls flyin' off the table, jumpin' over balls or nothin'. When he was clean, it was some beautiful shit to see. When he was strung out, his ass looked ridiculous. One time he jumped the cue ball off the table and broke out this big time dope dealer old lady's front teeth. He had to leave town over that shit for a minute. Eventually that nigga Tut squared shit with the motherfucker so he could come back home.

Tut put this little underground tournament together. He was trying to make a big name for himself. He had the best players comin' in from all over the country. Frisco, Memphis, Milwaukee, Buffalo, you name it. It cost twenty-five large to get in. Then you could take all the side bets, after hours action and hustlin' locals you could handle. The big payoff was $100Gs. If Pop wins he'll be off the hook for almost everything he owes Tut out of his half. If he loses he's gotta turn all kinds of tricks for Tut until they're square biz. That'll take forever.

The old man's got a good chance though. I haven't seen him play since I moved to Detroit a few years ago. The grapevine says he's been off that "Boy" for a minute now and his hands don't shake no mo'. They say he was so strung out a while back that he was snortin' "T's and B's" and livin' in the back of Smiley's. Then he met some church goin' lady a couple years ago who put him up in her attic 'til he kicked "King Heroin" cold turkey. When he's clean he can beat anybody on the planet. Everybody came to win this motherfucker though.

I've been around the country with this pool cue. I've whipped just about all of these cats ass before. A couple I've never seen. The rest can't be no better than the best though and I've beaten the best. Make no mistake about it, I came here to win. If Scratch ends up being the nigga whose ass I had to whip to get that money then so be it.

"Jo Jo!!!!! Come here nigga!!!! You done got too good to speak to yo' own Daddy!!!!????"

Loud and flashy, that was Scratch. I could see he took some of Tut's money and got himself some new "vines" too. His old lucky cranberry Borsalino hat with the pink band was the only old thing about him, except for the lines in his face and the tracks in his arms. In his new three-piece black mohair suit and burgundy Stacy Adams boots, he looked more like a player on a winning streak than a broken down hustler on the long comeback trail. I could see he was back to keepin' the wrong company too.

"Rip, you know my boy Jo-Jo don't you????"
"Good to see you Pop. Ya look good man. Rip, long time. Good ta see you too." I said with warmed over insincerity.

Rip was up from St. Louis. He was one helluva player. He would come to KC every once in a while after he'd whupped everybody's ass in St. Louis. Rip was serious competition. That wasn't the problem though. The trouble with Rip was that when he lost, which was rare, he'd try to start some shit rather than pay you your money. If he bet on your game on the side and you lost he'd want to fight you too. Either way, when Rip loss you didn't want to fuck with him.

Rip did 7 ½ years in Boonville for manslaughter. He beat this drunk motherfucker to death with a twelve ball for bumpin' against the table when he was shootin'. He woulda caught a 2nd degree murder case, but they say the judge and Rip's lawyer played pool together. I guess they could understand that shit. Pop would go watch Rip box when he was in prison. Scratch took action on the fights from the guards and would split his winnings with Rip.

"Long time???? Damn nigga, that's all you got to say to your Uncle Rip???? Shiiiit, I taught you every thang you know." He signified as he put his arm around my neck and spilled some of his Remy on my pants.

"Fuck you mean taught him everythang he know???? I taught this motherfucker everything he know. If you taught him anythang it'd be how I taught you how to take a good ass whuppin'" Scratch pronounced with all the confidence in the world.

"Nigga you must be crazy. You ain't never whupped my ass. Ain't never gone too long as you draw breath either." Rip let it be known.

"All right, all right. Don't you two old niggas go havin' a coronary up in here. Scratch you taught me everythang I knew…. I learned the rest from whuppin' Rip's ass." I said jokingly, but not sure it went over like I meant it too.

"You hear this nigga???? Rip chortled to Scratch. "Whuppin' Rip's ass" He said mockingly as he stuck out his chest and threw back the corner of cognac that was left in his glass. "This young nigga done got too big for his britches Scratch. Boy you come here to play or you jus' came to talk shit???? 'Cus we ain't gotta wait 'til no tournament. I can wax your young ass right now."

I knew it was time for me to go now. Thank God Smiley walked over from behind the bar to join in on the fellowship.

"What y'all two old loud ass niggas over here lying about now????" Smiley blurted out as he placed his meaty hands on their shoulders. "Jo-Jo, I know this ones yo' Daddy, but that other one there I'd stay clear of that motherfucker if I was you. Ain't no telling what's liable to happen when this nigga come 'round here. Jo-Jo, which one of these old niggas ass you gone have to beat to win that money????"

"I'm just gone play my game. If it's on, then it's on. We'll just have to see what happens." I said

"Jo-Jo, you ain't drinkin'???? Beefeater and grapefruit right????" Smiley asked anticipating a sale.

Everybody was on their hustle and Smiley's hustle was slingin' drinks. At the end of the day you never let nothin' take your mind off your hustle. Pop taught me that.

"I'm bout to get out of here Smiley, but you can buy these two "Gentlemen" whatever they drinkin' 'til this runs out." I said as a gesture of respect.

"Allright then Young Buck." Smiley accepted gladly and impressed as I handed him a hundred dollar bill.

"Look at him Scratch." Rip chimed in. "Now this nigga tryin' to peel big paper on us. Boy you somethin' else Young Blood."

"Leave him alone Rip. The boy all right. Thank you for the drink son. You stayin' at your Aunt Retha's????" Scratch inquired sounding like a concerned father.

"Yeah Pop, I'll be there 'til Monday"

"You tell my Sister I said I love her. I'll try to stop by there and see y'all tomorrow. Y'all need anything let me know."

"Okay Pop, see ya when I see ya. Rip, Smiley ya'll be easy. I'm gone go get me some sleep and some of Aunt Retha's ribs and cornbread so I can build up enough strength to come back up here and start kickin' ass and takin' names."

As I was headed out the door I could see Tut comin' out of Smiley's office. Over the years he had managed to get a piece of Smiley's club, which really turned out good for everybody. Shooting pool every day at Smiley's, was the closest thing Scratch was ever gonna have to a regular job. Tut had a permanent place to set up shop and Smiley would never lose his club to the other dope pushers. Tut had a hand in just about everything in KC, but he treated Smiley's like it was the center of his empire.

I couldn't wait to get to the house. I couldn't wait to see Aunt Retha. Retha was Daddy's little sister. She was the youngest, but she was about the only one in the family who ever kept a square job. Their brother was pullin' a twenty-five year bid for armed robbery in El Dorado, Kansas. Their sister Margie Jean was bout like mama. She lived in Oklahoma City and slept from pillar to post layin' up with whatever old dude would put up with her.

Aunt Retha was an angel though. She was always good to me and made sure I stayed out of trouble. I never felt like she was just sorry for me because of my mama and daddy. I always felt like she loved me like I was her own child.

Retha never married. If she had a boyfriend I never knew about it. She didn't seem to have time for a man between her job, taking care of me, her church and taking care of her house.

That house seemed like what she loved more than anything. I never really knew how a single woman managed to buy such a big house, or why she needed such a big house in the first place. It was just me and her for the longest time. We were happy together.

Sometimes daddy would stay with us a few days at a time. As soon as he shacked up with some new chick he was gone. Margie Jean stayed with us for almost a year when she was running away from somebody or something. Most of the time it was just me and Aunt Retha.

She always had some kind of company over to the house though. There was usually some woman sittin' up in the parlor crying on Auntee's shoulder about how her man had left her, or some slick church Deacon sittin' in the living room trying to sweet talk his way onto the deed to Retha's house. I ain't never asked her who she was leaving it too. It probably don't matter though, since I expect she'll live longer than all of us. As I opened the gate and crossed the footpath to the stairs, I could feel home settle in one me.

I wish I had come here first instead of going to check in over at Smiley's. I couldn't help but think about Scratch and the trouble he was gonna be in if he lost Tut's investment. I must admit, this tournament was some slick shit Tut had put together. He was gonna be

"The Man" after this shit was over wit'.

"The Best of the Best Kansas City Nine Ball Tournament" He brought together 44 players for a four day tournament at $25k a pop for a best five out of nine 9 Ball tournament. He was gonna make a million dollars after he paid out the hundred g's and then he was in on all the pussy being sold, the liquor and he had a piece of all the other action. As an added bonus, he would have the services of Kansas City's best smack junkie pool hustler at his service for the rest of his days if Pop lost.

When I saw him comin' out of the office earlier, it seemed like he wasn't as happy as a Black man about to make a million dollars should be though. Tut was always a mean lookin' motherfucker, but he looked more scared than pissed off to me. None of that necessarily had anything to do with Scratch, but since they were probably about to go into business together for life, whatever Tut was into, Scratch would be into right wit' him from now on. Like Pop always told me though, when I didn't have a shot and all of my balls was blocked behind his "You got yo'self in this shit boy, now lemme see you get yo' ass out of it."

"Jo-Jo!!!! Have you seen yo' Daddy????" She asked before my suitcase had a chance to stop rockin'

"Damn Aunt Retha, good to see you too. Can I get in the door first???? – I Love you too. Yeah I seen him, down at Smiley's a l'il bit ago."

"Child you just don't know. That woman of his done called her fifty-eleven times lookin'
for that man and since she's such a Christian woman she can't take her big ass down to
Smiley's and look' for him herself."

"What woman????" I asked.

"Fannie Jones, yo' Daddy's girlfriend" She stated incredulously "Boy come here and give
me some sugar. Why'd you go down to that damn club instead of comin' home first???? I
fixed you some ham steak, candied yams and collard greens but they cold now. Got me
sittin' up here doin' all this cookin' and worryin' 'bout y'all"

"I had to sign in." I answered. "I'll just heat it up. What's Daddy's girlfriend doin' callin'
here." I asked in between the big hug and kiss I had been waiting for.

"She don't want Scratch to play in that damn tournament. Said she had a vision that
somethin' bad was gone happen to him. "Spiritual Visions." She scoffed. "I remember
when that heifer used to have a house full of niggas playin' dominoes on Sunday." She
remembered fondly. "Let me go in here and fix you this plate. Come in here and sit
down."

"I remember Miss Fannie. That's pop's church lady????" I chuckled.

"Yes Lord and I thank her from the bottom of my heart for getting' yo' Daddy off that stuff. I just hope she know she ain't never gone get him to put that pool stick down. To be honest with you, I ain't that happy about neither one of y'all bein' mixed up in nothin' that damn no good nigga Tut got anything to do with."

"Auntee I'm just gone make this money, catch up with my favorite Aunt for a few days, then take my Black ass back to Detroit where the women know how to cook." I teased.

"Child please. I'll rake this plate out the back door and let the dogs get it if you don't hush." She said as she reached for my plate.

"No, no, no, no, no. I'm sorry Mama. You know you the best cook in Kansas City. Can you hand me a cold beer please????"

"Yo' feet don't look broke to me." She said as she kissed me on the forehead. "Child I'm going up to my bed. It's too late to be worryin' about grown folks. If that woman call back over here, will you tell her you seen yo' Daddy and he must not been the one she saw in the vision????" She asked jokingly. "Take that plate out the oven in 'bout five minutes."

"Okay Aunt Retha. Can you hand me the hot sauce before you go up????" I asked just to mess with her. "Boy leave me alone. I'll see you in the morning. I love you Sugar." "I love you too Aunt Retha." I said.

Good family, good food, cold beer and a good night's sleep in a warm house. What more could a Black man ask for. I just hoped Aunt Retha wasn't gonna let Fannie's foolish visions about Daddy keep her from having sweet dreams. I know I'm gonna sleep good tonight. You can best believe that.

Bam Bam Bam Bam!!!!
Bam Bam Bam Bam!!!!
Bam Bam Bam Bam!!!!

"What the hell" I can't believe nobody would be knocking on Aunt Retha's door this early in the morning. I must be dreaming. I picked up my watch off the nightstand and saw that it's only 5:37am. Now I know it must have been a dream, since ain't nobody crazy enough to be knockin' on her door this early in the morning. She would curse their ass out 'til the Devil had to cover his ears. I close my eyes and try to get back to sleep.

"Lawd Have Mercy Jesus!!!!!" Retha screamed.

Vince Vanguard Vainglorious

Vainglorious Press 2007

Transit

....Black, fat and ugly - Do she have to be eatin' them bright red hot sauce drippin' wings on the train too????

Please let yo' li'l girl have one so she'll stop cryin' – Pleeeeze

....Grease all over her mouth - Lookin' like ghetto lip gloss

Jus' had to sit next to a White man too - makin' us all look bad....

Lord have mercy Jesus

Y'all try not to look at her - Please.....

....Look at her - Leanin' all up in her seat like she want you to see her.

Jus' a hot mess....

cd's...dvd's...cd's....dvd's....

....I bet she one a them "College Girls"

Them ho's ain't shit – Steppin' all over my new shoes!!!!

What she doin' on the train anyway????

I bet that ain't her real hair

I can't stand them ho's!!!!

They thank they all that

I'll be glad when she get off this train

She bett'not look at me again neither

Forgive me Lord

....I can't stand them ho's!!!!

....oils....incense....oils...incense

....Lord have mercy, I can't wait to tell my roommate about this hoochie here

Blue hair, pink nails and a red thong

I can't wait to get me a car and get away from these Black folks

Child they a mess

Ain't no tellin' how many babies she got

What's that smell????

Lord please let me off this train....

socks....footies....socks....footies

....Lord, Please don't let that Nigga sit next to me

Damn!!!! Why every day some dirty construction job Nigga gotta sit next to me????

Where all the men with the "good" jobs at????

No I don't look familiar, so please don't ask....

Lord, Please let me get to my stop before another Blue Collar Nigga try to talk to me

got that green....got that hard....got that green....got that hard....

Po' child, his mama must didn't see him leave the house this mo'nin'

Lord why don't that child pull up his pants????? Draw's all showin'

Look at that - the girls got they tails all hangin' out too....Oooh child - a thong

....Don't they mama's teach 'em nothin' no mo'????

"Oh....Thank you baby - Mama sho' do need to sit down today"

I'll keep prayin' for 'em Jesus, they still yo' chillun

....cd's.....dvd's....cd's...dvd's

Vince Vanguard Vainglorious

Vainglorious Press 2006

Vince Rogers was raised in **Atlanta**'s infamous **Bowen Homes** housing projects. After graduating with distinction from **Frederick Douglass High School**, he went on to attend prestigious **Morehouse College** on an academic scholarship. He has been active in community development and economic empowerment organizations for over twenty years. He is also an accomplished economist, specializing in urban development and international economics.

As a child he attended historic **Ebenezer Baptist Church.** He was baptized by the honorable **Reverend Martin Luther King Sr. -** "Daddy King". He was highly influenced by the spiritual, cultural and social teachings of the church. Those ideals have inspired him to work to make the world a better place to live.

He is an internationally published writer of fiction, non-fiction, poetry, feature articles, film criticism and scholarly papers. His works were among the Official Inaugural Selections of *"I've Known Rivers"* the **Museum of the African Diaspora** story project. He was the **TimBookTu Featured Writer** for December of 2006. His scholarly paper *The Evolution of Shawntae Harris* was presented at **Vanderbilt University**'s "Smoke, Lilies & Jade" Lecture **Series** during the **Hip Hop's Defiant Divas Conference.**

He has also contributed to: **Clean Sheets Magazine; On The Black Burner; Taj Mahal Review; Chicken Bones: A Journal; Thereby Hangs a Tale; Catalyst Magazine; Book Club News; Southern Screen Report; Pulp Magazine; Nghosi Books: <u>Longing Lust and Love Anthology</u>; 3 Lights Gallery; Black Arts Quarterly; Amistad Journal**

Also available @ <u>www.lulu.com</u> **Wax Vainglorious**: the Collected Works of li'l boy and Josephine's baby boy **Volume 2**; The Poetry of Shake Speare Chucker

"I have nothing to declare except my genius."

Oscar Wilde

www.ingramcontent.com/pod-product-compliance
Lightning Source LLC
Chambersburg PA
CBHW051825170626
46807CB00003B/1039